Covenant Roman Catholic

Church

Sterling Forks Tennessee

Jon Hykes

To FRANK

12/21/2016

To Father Edward Chadziewitz

Who welcomed me and took my confession

Who came to me in a dream and gave me this story

Of love

Of Identity

Of Reconciliation

And Redemption

A sequel to:

Who's Going to Say *Kaddish* for the

Chinaman's Dog

A love story set in South Central Tennessee

A Story about

Identity

Foreword

When the Calvinists were expelled from Great Britain they, like many other persecuted religious minorities came to America. Many of these Scotch Irish Calvinists settled in the Southern Appalachian Mountains. Much of our musical tradition comes from these people. They sent out missionaries all through the region. The Cherokee embraced Calvinism because the tenet of predestination squared neatly with their beliefs and soon every little Cherokee hamlet had a little white frame church with a small steeple above the front door. When the Cherokee Nation was forcibly relocated to Oklahoma, all these little churches were abandoned, as nobody wanted to worship in a church that the Indians used. Eventually after the Civil War some of them were adopted by black Southern Baptist congregations. If you look around the Mid-South you will still find some of these little church buildings out in the country.

Some of them were adopted by the Grange. Some of
them were lived in as residences. This is the story of
one of those little churches at the end of the Twentieth
Century

The Game With No Name

There is a game.

It has no name.

It's played by one and all,

There is a game

That has no name.

It's played by Great and small.

There is a game.

It has no name.

All the players

Are unaware.

There is a game.

It has no name.

The rules change

From day to day.

There is a game.

It has no name.

It's played so unaware.

There is a game

It has no name.

The players don't even care.

There is a game.

It has no name.

Name it if you dare.

There is a game.

It has no name.

It has to be played the same.

Or in that game,

That has no name,

The odd one gets expelled.

To play that game,

That has no name.

You must follow every rule;

Because to play that game,

That has no name,

One has to be a fool.

1

Fred Katz was sitting on his sofa, proof reading press releases for his new book. It was obvious that the people in marketing hadn't read it. The body of the press release didn't match the aim or tone of the book at all. Marketing probably hadn't read his other book either, as the information about past work had about a five percent accuracy rating. He couldn't complain about it, because the marketing people made his modest Gothic pot boiler a best seller. He was counting lines and penciling words on the correction sheet, trying to remember the rules from The Associated Press Style Book, without actually getting up and opening it.

"Shit, he muttered to himself, it was easier to write the thing than it is to sell it."

The pile of paper on the sofa slid to the floor. The other marketing documents were there too. Some were copies of stuff he'd already finished, and others were permission forms to send releases to give the other book another push. He picked up the pile and resorted it. Halfway through the pile there was a knock at the door. He got up and looked through the peep hole. He didn't see anyone. There was another knock while he was looking through the peep hole, and it dawned on him that it was Marjorie. She was standing close to the door again. He opened the door and let her in.

"What's that pile of paper?

"Publicity stuff, It's all a pain in the ass. I forgot all about it after the first book took off."

"Doesn't the publisher do all that stuff?"

"The publisher does a lot. This is the stuff that for one reason or another, the publisher can't, or won't do."

"Like what?"

"Well, there's fact checking the personal pieces in the press releases. The guys in marketing don't know me from Adam. Most of the time, they haven't even read the book that they're selling."

"How do you sell something without knowing anything about it?"

"Madison Avenue does it every day."

"They do?"

"How many men do you know that use feminine hygiene products- Madison Avenue is mainly a male bastion. Women do office work and serve coffee."

"I never thought of that."

"Every piece of copy there has two pieces of paper attached to it. One is the correction sheet, and the other is the permission sheet for when the corrections are made so it can be used."

"But there's a lot of paper there."

Covenant Roman Catholic Church

"That's nationwide narrow cast ad campaigns for two books, calculated for impact by market research."

"What does Narrow cast mean?"

"By individual locality. Houston and Chicago are two totally different places. Marketing emphasizes different things for the different places reflecting regional and ethnic tastes."

"But how do the copywriters do it if they never saw the book?"

"I tell them in as few words as possible what the book is about. They go from there. The fun part is condensing 300 or so pages into two or three sentences."

"I never looked at it that way before."

"Anyway, what brings you to my humble abode?"

"Well... Remember when I went to the synagogue with you?"

Covenant Roman Catholic Church

"Yeah, we were all glad that you came. You made Minyan possible, so we could be within the Law."

"I want to ask a similar favor. I haven't been to Mass since nursing school. Father Bob feels that I need to start going again so I can remain in a state of Grace. He mumbled something about Divine intervention on my confession. He also said something about an awakening. Anyway, he wants me there. I don't know a soul in that church. Could you come with me? Charlene is still out at Ben's place."

"I have never been in a church. I wouldn't know what to do."

"You'll be OK, just do what I do."

"I don't know..."

"I went to synagogue with you. I had no clue, but I did it anyway."

"I'd stick out as an outsider."

"Just lose the hat. I'm an outsider too. The only person there I know is Father Bob, and I really don't know him."

"I've seen him in the diner. He seems friendly enough, but I'm still Jewish, and there has been an enmity between Catholics and Jews for over a thousand years."

"You don't go to Synagogue very often"

"I haven't felt welcome since my divorce. I still give them money every year."

"You guys don't even have a regular Rabbi. You have trouble mustering a Minyan...I did say it right, didn't I?"

"Yeah, you did, but up until 1976, this was a Southern Baptist college town with a big Congregational Church. I never could figure that one out."

Covenant Roman Catholic Church

"According to people around here, Reverend Sterling got a deal on land here. The Congregational church was here before the Civil War."

"But Sterling Forks?"

"This area used to be the Sterling plantation. They tried to grow cotton, but the soil wasn't up to it. They bankrupted before the Civil War, and moved out. The name stuck though. Reverend Sterling and Sterling Forks is just a coincidence."

"How did you learn so much about the town?"

"New employee orientation at the college. All employees have to know that stuff."

"How come I didn't get the course?"

"Were you an employee, on the books?"

"I was an adjunct professor."

"Did they take out Social Security and withhold

Taxes?"

"No."

Covenant Roman Catholic Church

"You were an outside contractor."

"I guess that's my lot- always the outsider."

"We're both outsiders. Are you going to
Church with me or not?"

Yeah, I guess so."

2 Sid's Visitor

"Sir, I know that trying to drown myself in the toilet was stupid, but it's the only way I can get any attention here."

"Couldn't you just have asked a guard?"

"I never come in contact with any guards. All I see are trustees. They bring me food, clean clothing, Vaseline and depends."

"Why didn't you talk to them?"

"They shove it in through the slot and are gone before I can say anything. "

"How long has this been going on?"

Except for the visitor I had, a couple of weeks ago, I have had no human contact since I've been here.

"You're not in solitary, you're in a cell block. How do you not have any contact?

" There's nobody in any of the other cells."

"I can't believe that. We are letting people out because of over-crowding, and we have an empty cell block reserved for one inmate?"

"That's what I just told you."

"And you never see any guards?"

"They use a T V camera. When I get dehydrated and pass out, I lay on the floor for hours before any one comes to investigate."

"But you had a visitor."

"Yeah, the first...Ever! Look, Mr. Warden, I have been in the system on and off for twenty-seven years. I know that I'm going to die here. I know that I truly deserve to be here. People on the outside are happy to have me here. Every time I have been here, I have made myself unwelcome by being a total fuck-up. It's a miracle that I am alive. The guards should have killed me years ago. I deserve it! Hell, I can't even kill myself. The people here would be glad if I did. That includes both the guards and the other inmates. "

Covenant Roman Catholic Church

"Yes, I've read your record. You've done everything on the outside except Capital Felony murder. You have never been outside for more than a year since you were sixteen. You have put four guards on disability and seriously injured sixteen other inmates. You have done a total of seven years in segregation and three in the hole. How am I supposed to believe that you have turned over a new leaf and want to redeem yourself?"

"I never had a visitor before."

"Never?"

"Just an occasional public defender."

"No family?"

"I ran away for the last time when I was twelve. My asshole was sore."

" No friends?"

"Think about it sir... I spent four years in juvie until I got nailed for strong arm robbery two days after I was released to a foster home."

"How am I to know that this isn't a scam to get something from us?"

"The visitor is the person that caused me to be a null."

"A null?"

"Yeah, No sexual organs at all."

"Yeah, I heard about your... uh...condition."

"I had it coming."

"Why did she come to visit you?"

"She wanted to apologize. She wanted me to forgive her."

"Did you?"

"She forgave me for raping her and leaving her naked and unconscious in the middle of a public park."

"She was one of your victims?"

"Yeah, from the time before last that I was on the outside... Two months later I got caught in the middle of a home invasion."

Covenant Roman Catholic Church

"Why aren't you in here for that?"

"There was a kilo of coke on the coffee table
when they came to arrest me. His shotgun went off
in the struggle, and a neighbor called the cops. I
skated on a technicality and only spent a year and a
half in jail for pretrial confinement. Hell, I should be
dead!"

"With your record you got caught in a home
invasion.... and got off?"

"I am being kept alive for some reason. Hell,
I've lost count of the times I've tried to kill myself."

"And you forgave her."

"Look, Sir, She did this to me because of
what I did to her. I'm three times her size. I don't
even remember when I did it to her, I did it to a lot
of women over the years. Until she showed up, I
never even felt guilty about it. Then I realized that
until I make up for at least some of what I have
done, I can't even die. Face it, Sir, my life is truly
hell. I can't stand for more than five minutes or I get

21

dehydrated, I can't sit because the insides of my legs and my ass are too sore. There is no position where I'm comfortable. I leak, so I have to have a plastic-coated mattress and no bedding. I have a constant headache, and I have lost almost half my body weight. On top of it all, I smell bad, so nobody wants to be around me. I brought this all on myself. All I can do is act as a warning to others. I owe it to everybody. " "Look, there isn't much I can do in the system that will improve your situation. I don't think that there's anything anybody can do, but I can't allow you to kill yourself, any more than I can allow anybody else to kill you. You're right about dying here. It's going to happen. I can't help the medical situation, or the smell. I'm going to try to find a program for you, but if you screw it up, you will spend the rest of your life in the hole."

The walk back to his cell exhausted Sid. His depend was leaking and digestive juices were pooling inside his shoes. Worse yet, he had a whole day wait for his next shower. He got showers three times a week. For a normal inmate that was fine, but with his special needs, it was very hard to clean up after leaks, and this leak was both bad, and anticipated. Counting travel time and the time in the office, he had been vertical for two and a half hours, so the entire contents of his alimentary tract was in the depend. It took him half an hour to clean himself from the leak and another fifteen minutes to clean up the mess on the floor from having the depend off to clean himself up. He fell into his bunk and went violently to sleep.   If Sid's waking world was hell, there was no temporal or biblical description of his dreams. Since Marjorie's visit, they happened more frequently, and more vividly. He was always five or six years old, and back home in Memphis. His pants were gone, and he had blood on the insides of both of his legs and he was crying to his mother about the last session with dear old Dad in the living room. She was crying too, but wouldn't pick him up or hold him, or even clean off the blood. She had a large red hand print on the side of her face. This was the tail end of the dream. This was after being beaten and sodomized, and being called a worthless piece of shit, that was alive only because dear old Dad couldn't figure a failure proof way of disposing of a child's body. Dear old Dad had left, and his mother was staring blankly into space, crying quietly. Anger, shame, revulsion, and dread filled his soul as he jerked awake.   He was safe here in prison. The last person that tried to sodomize him here was also the first. He was still drooling in a convalescent home mentally incapable of ever sodomizing anyone else again. Three of the four guards that pulled Sid off the other inmate had permanent scars from the encounter. Sid still had a lump on his nose and a distorted eye socket. Nobody ever tried anything else on Sid. He lay on his bunk and reflected on the last couple of weeks. His meeting with Marjorie had awakened things inside him. Some of them he had buried intentionally, and some of them he had never experienced before. It was the first truly civil meeting he had ever had with a woman. There was no fear nor anger from neither him nor her. They just talked. She was sympathetic toward him- not like the many social workers from his past, but human being to human being. There was no agenda, or hidden meaning to the conversation. It was a sharing of past experience. She told him what she had done to him, and expressed regret at what she had done. She brought up their encounter in the past and forgave him for it. She told him about her anger and pain over years, and the feeling of shame and worthlessness the experience caused and what she had done to others and her regrets about that. Here and there, an occasional tear was shed as she told her tale. He could tell it was hard for her to do it. He had casually taken something irreplaceable from her, and destroyed it. He had done it without even really

Covenant Roman Catholic Church

thinking about it or really remembering it. Then while he was trying to put everything into logical places she forgave him for what he had done to her. To her, he wasn't the monster everyone else saw, but another suffering human being. She asked him to forgive her. She, who had maimed and disfigured him, and made him totally dependent on the State of Tennessee Department of Corrections. She who reduced his gender to marks on a piece of paper.......She who cared about him as a human being, something even his parents failed to do. She whose life was turned upside down by his irrational act of rage. She who forgave him for it and all it meant to the world; except for one chance collision, a stranger, she forgave him. It shocked him to the center of his being. She did it without drama, without ceremony, just one person to another. She collected a portion of the vast debt that he owed countless women over a period of years. It was a justified collection. He reconciled instantly to it, because he knew he had it coming multiple times over. In doing so she represented all the women he damaged over the years, and as their representative, she forgave him. He started to cry for the first time since he was a small boy and his mother couldn't or wouldn't help him or get him out of there. Between sobs, he forgave her... The guards led him back to his cell and locked the door behind him. As he cleaned himself from the half hour in a semi vertical position, he tried to rationalize it all. All his life he was the person that wasn't worth the trouble of killing, forgiven by a stranger that he had preyed upon. He tried to drown himself in the toilet. He forced two used depends into the trap and held the button down until it filled to the top. He stuck his head in as far as he could and inhaled. He woke up three hours later on his side on the floor beside the toilet. His chest hurt. He had a terrible taste in his mouth and a big bump on his head. He had failed again. He knew that the guards had seen it. There were two cameras pointing into his cell. He crawled

to his bunk and climbed on. He needed to talk to

someone. For the first time in his life, he had worth.

6 L&N

Following the tragic death of Chet by heart attack in the locomotive cab, the awkward and cumbersome selection process of engineer selection went into motion. Promotion of a fireman to the position of engineer was loaded with office politics, government regulation and union work rules. There were no more replacement engineers. Chet's temporary replacement was waiting to retire. When Chet came back, he retired. He'd put off retirement for almost a year, and his family didn't want to wait any more. There were sixteen candidates for three engineer slots. Two were job applicants from other rail roads, and the others were all senior firemen. Judge Green missed the seniority cut by six months even though he got a perfect score on the test for engineer. Ten senior firemen flunked the test. One Hispanic senior fireman was promoted even though he had the lowest test score. He had the seniority, and was superior in work ethic and ability on the job. There also was a diversity push from the Federal Government. At the end of the six-week selection process, Doug ended up back on the Nashville to Mobile run, sharing the cab with Judge Green. The twenty per cent pay increase didn't make up for the massive overtime pay he got as a substitute, but it came close. In the bargain, he got a fireman that he admired and respected, because Judge knew the paperwork and regulations better than he did. Neither man was terribly happy with the assignment, as that particular run was the longest on the line and had the heaviest volume. It also meant overnight away from home.   The cab of the locomotive was a good place for Doug. Home was a battleground. In the locomotive, things were more or less predictable. Things on the train would break. Things on other trains would break. An occasional tree would fall across the track or there would be a washout somewhere. Events on the train had no additional baggage. Delays meant overtime. The new locomotives for the long runs had air conditioning. No more sweltering through the summer. Best of all, the railroad was making a profit, so there were many improvements on the roadbed. Most of the rail was welded, and the mechanical joints necessary for expansion and contraction were staggered and made a huge difference in the noise in the cab. That little improvement also meant higher speeds and shorter travel times.

On the home front for Doug, things were terrible. His mother in law inserted herself between him and his wife. This made honest communication between them impossible, as if Doug made any attempt at correction or criticism, she would immediately call Mama and complain about what a bad person her husband was. That is where the restraining order came from. Everything now had to go through Social Services, the marriage counselor, or the court. He couldn't even take the baby out of the house without an escort. What passed for housework before stopped completely. The baby was now two years old and fully ambulatory. Child protective services was fully involved in the case. There were three attorneys involved. Julie's mother insisted that her daughter was a good wife and mother, in spite of the mountain of evidence to the contrary. Julie's mother stood between the idea of her being a good wife and mother and reality, painful as it was. There was never a divorce in Doug's family, and Doug didn't want to be the first.

Since the train wreck at Sterling Forks, and Chet's heart attack several months later, Doug felt a certain discomfort with that particular stretch of track. He felt s certain chill occasionally as he passed the crossing for Huntsville Pike. Because of a couple of scandals on other railroads, the televisions were banned from the cabs of locomotives. Doug knew from his experience in Sterling Forks, that the lack of a television would have not made any difference in the accident at the crossing. Both men were watching the track. Judge and Doug were watching the track now too, as nothing at all was happening. The heavy freight traffic was taking a toll on the tracks and it was necessary to pay attention for the slightest variations to report before they were bad enough to cause a derailment. Some of the ties in the roadbed were placed when the railroad was using steam locomotives, so anchor plates were an important thing to look at, even at thirty miles an hour. Washouts were another thing to look out for. Around the towns along the line there was some vandalism here and there as people stole the wiring from the signals and occasional anchor plates. All those things needed to be reported as quickly as possible to avoid delays later on. When there were delays, the lack of a television made them seem longer. Judge made the delays easier to bear as he had a quick wit about him and also understood the things Doug was going through at home.

"She's bored. That's the problem," said Judge one afternoon."

"I can't see how that could be" said Doug as he was scribbling down yet another roadbed damage report.

"It's really simple. She's with a preschooler 24/7 and a television."

7 Little White Church

The Covenant Roman Catholic Church building started life as The Sterling Covenant Church which was a sect of the Calvinist movement of the 1780's. It was a small white clapboard church building on a native stone foundation. It had three tall windows on each side and a stubby little bell tower above the front vestibule. The bell disappeared during the war effort of World War II. At the time, the building was being used as a Grange hall. When the Sterling Forks Grange built their new hall in 1955, it was used for storage by the Grange. When Sterling Bible College went Liberal Arts, the building was donated to the small Catholic congregation that formed among the newcomers to the college. It was an intimate little church. It had six pews on each side of the aisle. On one side of the Altar was the Sacristy, and the other held the confessional. The local music store donated an H3 Hammond organ which sat against the Sacristy wall.

To do this they had to cut five feet off the front pew. It was a Jesuit Mission Church in its purest form. The town knew it as the Covenant Church, so the name stayed. Father Bob was the only Priest and he came with the consecration of the building. He was from Baltimore, and was ordained at a mission in Cameroon, where he was a missionary. In Cameroon, he baptized over a thousand people in the ten years he served as a priest there. He really didn't want to leave, but his little mission church became a full-fledged Church, and the Order wanted him back in the USA to train and recruit missionaries. After a year of this, he wanted to function as a Priest again as he was feeling a little bit of alienation. He couldn't really describe the feeling, but he needed to celebrate Mass more. When the little congregation in Tennessee petitioned for a priest, he jumped at the chance. The area hadn't even been incorporated as a parish. The nearest parish was Lynchburg and the next nearest was Huntsville. He was truly a missionary priest again, carrying The Holy Spirit to people hungry to receive it. Until the building was ready, he lived with Earl and Molly and celebrated Mass in their living room. There had never been a Mass celebrated in Sterling Forks before. Father Bob and his Message were warmly received by the small congregation. However, a single man living an ascetic lifestyle professing the Roman Faith was looked upon as odd by the rest of the town. Catholics were on TV but not in the Bible belt. A Jesuit missionary was, well, strange.

The local clerics figured it out first. Here was a man that embodied the things that they preached about, and prayed for. He was living the Gospel. He wasn't doing it for show, but just doing it. Here was the real deal. None of them had any idea about Catholic Doctrine or Dogma, much less Tradition. To them the Divine Mysteries were mysteries. To them, the Holy Spirit was something that other people experienced, but wasn't something that was present in everyday life. It gave snake handlers the ability to handle snakes and occasional cripples the ability to walk at revivals. Those revival miracles were viewed with a certain amount of suspicion. They watched him very carefully. Father Bob's congregation aroused a certain amount of curiosity from the townspeople. Some of them were folks that lived there all their lives and went to Church in Lynchburg, but never said anything about which church. Others were students and employees of the college. There were about fifty people more or less. About a dozen were regulars at Mass. That faithful dozen or so were all that were needed to establish a Church. It took about six months to convert the old Grange Hall back into a Church. It took another month to find an Archbishop willing to help consecrate it. The ceremony was beautiful. The old church became a Church again. The ceremony was done a Capella, with the Mass celebrated by the Arch Bishop from Birmingham.

Covenant Roman Catholic Church

The plain little white Church glowed. They had a pot luck picnic in the yard afterward. The three people from the Order never showed up, but sent their regrets and their blessings. The Covenant Roman Catholic Church was now a living breathing being. For better or worse, Father Bob had his Calling.

After everyone left, Father Bob knelt at the Altar.

"Dear Lord: Thank you for giving this mission to us. We truly need it.

Thank you for the help which always shows up just when it's needed,

And is always just what is needed.

Keep us all mindful of all that is in Your Teachings, Promise, and Blessings.

Give us the strength to stand out as a beacon to bring the lost to your Home.

Give me the strength of faith every day to minister to them as they need without complaint or Question.

Give me the strength to be an example and embody all that is You, Father Son and Holy Spirit.

Continue flowing into the Eucharist here as in every other place where your Sacrifice is celebrated.

If I ever waver guide my faltering steps, for I am imperfect and cannot always do as I should.

I am here to do Thy Will for as long as it is Thy Will for me to do it.

In the Name of:

The Father

The Son

And

The Holy Spirit

Amen"

Covenant Roman Catholic Church

He crossed himself, rose, and walked back to Earl
and Molly's place.

8 the Homecoming

Chet came to himself on the platform of a strange railroad depot. A very familiar blonde woman and a sailor were sitting on the platform beside him. The depot was built of stone. It wasn't field stone, but what looked to be fine white marble. It looked like it was brand new, but it also looked like it had been there forever. He tried hard to process this new scene, but failed in the attempt. A couple of minutes ago, he had been in the cab of a locomotive suffering from terrible pains in his chest, jaw and left arm. Now he felt better than he could ever remember feeling. The area surrounding the depot was strangely familiar, but totally alien as well. The woman was wearing a red full skirted party dress with a Christmas motif. The Sailor was wearing his winter blues, with the stripes of a junior petty officer. They sat there waiting.

Covenant Roman Catholic Church

"Where am I?

"You're at the Depot", said the woman in the red dress.

"Yes, I can see that it's a depot, but I don't remember getting off a train here"

"Were you just on a train?

"Uh, yes."

"Well, this is the Depot."

"What depot is this? No railroad I ever saw would build a depot out of prime marble. It's just too expensive. Depots are built out of wood, or in some instances, brick. I've never seen a marble one before, and this one is way too clean to be beside a railroad track."

"Which depot this is isn't important. This is where we were told to meet you to take you home."

"Where, Nashville?"

"No, Home!"

"Now I am lost. I live in Nashville, Just off Donnellson Pike."

"That's where you lived, but....."

"What do you mean by but?"

"We have a message for you."

"Oh?

"Remember what was going on in the locomotive cab this afternoon?"

"Uhh...Yeah, but where are you going with it?"

"Well, we met you the first time at a grade crossing outside of Sterling Forks. Because of your reaction, we were chosen to meet you so you could see that there are no hard feelings here."

"O K........ Were you in a little blue car on Huntsville Pike?"

"That was us."

"I am so sorry...... It happened so fast. I feel terrible about it!"

Covenant Roman Catholic Church

"We saw it. We talked to you through your dreams and tried to tell you it's all OK."

"I remember a couple of times......You're the lady in the newspaper. I got it. The last dream had chest pains in it. I woke up in a cold sweat."

"We're taking you home, to the beginning/ the end. Your body is still in the locomotive. Judge Green has called for help and has stopped and is trying to revive you with CPR. However, your heart is in too bad a shape. It is time to go home, your parents are waiting for you."

"How ironic, I died of a broken heart."

"Yeah, I guess you did."

"Now that I am dead, what do I do? Where do I go?"

"First, we will reunite you with loved ones, then we go check your bets."

"Bets?"

"Yeah, bets. When you return here, after you are reunited with those who came back first, we check your bets about your life in the earthly plane of existence.

Covenant Roman Catholic Church

"I really don't understand now. Do you say there's gambling involved?"

"Yeah, we all bet on how long we can last in that environment and what finally kills us." "How does that work?" "If you predict how your life turns out and live out the predicted span, you get a new bet on a new person. If you lose, you have to go back and do it over again. If you do it perfectly, you don't have to go back at all if you don't want to, and stay here. For some reason, nobody wants to stay here. About six people have done it perfectly. They are allowed to come and go as they please. Then there the ones that never make it past birth. They come right back. The first available pregnancy after you make your bet, down you go as we say here. We even send some people back when we feel that they had a fighting chance of making improvements down there, or learning an important lesson for all of us. Some people come back three or four times in one life.

"Could I go back now if I wanted to?"

"No, you dealt with all the problems in that life in a heroic manner. Not only that, but you got a handle on an unsolvable. Everyone was watching you. Jolene was supposed to get pregnant and have a baby with enormous medical needs. Your pictures caused the relationship that was going to cause the pregnancy to unravel. You got rid of Billy Bob without killing him. There were heavy side bets. Not only that, if you die from a broken heart, you cannot go back into that life. I am afraid that our momentary lapse of reason, ethics and propriety caused that. For that we are both sorry."

"What lapse?

"I had the drunken urge to tear Dave's clothes off. It happened as we were approaching the grade crossing. I guess it was bad timing on our parts. Dave got distracted and didn't hear the approaching train. The Depot was our way of making it up to you. We came in through the tunnel like most other people do. We caused your broken heart. We also made it possible for you to break the unsolvable. The time off for your trauma gave you time to figure it out. You had a good twenty years left. Maybe not so good because of the disabled baby, but twenty years anyway.

"How do you know that?"

"We looked up the original script and the bets on it."

"Now I am lost. There is a script...... and bets?

"The Presbyterians call it predestination."

"You are telling me I was working from a script?"

"Sort of...... When you go down, you are given several native abilities, and a gift. As you pass through the portal into a baby, the trauma of being born erases most of your memory of past lives and the experience here, as well as the names of the abilities and the gift. You have to discover those things as you grow. If you are lucky, the memory of past gender is erased as well. If you are not, it adds another burden to solve during your allotted three score and ten. The burdens are the uncontrollable circumstances of your birth, as you have no choice as to the baby you inhabit, not even gender. You just drop in to the next available baby, shortly after conception. That is what the bets are about. It's whether or not you can get past the three score and ten, and learn the lessons. It's about finding the gift and using it to its best benefit. It's how you use your innate abilities and compensate for accidents of birth. After you go down there, it's all up to you, regardless of where you're born."

As they walked down the path from the depot, the ground started slanting gradually upward and the path turned to compensate for the slope. Eventually the slope turned vertical and the path ran along the foot of the slope. After a distance, they came to a portal in the hill. It was ancient rough cut gray granite. The path led into the tunnel. A feeling of calmness and euphoria cam over him as they entered the tunnel. It led upward and turned gently to the left. As they walked through the tunnel Chet felt all the stress and cares of a lifetime of hardscrabble existence drain from his soul. All the worries disappeared. As they walked and turned, he sensed a light up ahead. As they approached the light it got brighter. It wasn't a painful brightness, but a brightness of clean and newness. He heard voices. They were happy voices. Some of them were voices he hadn't heard since his childhood. They were friendly voices, comforting voices. It was like walking into a pot luck supper in a church basement, but it also had the hum of a busy casino. There was a banner saying WELCOME HOME hanging form two poles. There were hundreds of people there, every one of them happy to see him. Chet was happy too. He had never in recent memory felt so happy and contented. He looked at his traveling companions. Miranda who was a middle aged blonde woman was now a child of about ten as was Dave. He looked at his hands and saw that he too was about ten, plus or minus a year. He remembered a Bible verse he heard as a child.

Matthew 18 verse 3:

"And said "Verily I say unto you, except ye repent and become as little children, ye shall not enter the kingdom of Heaven."

Everything made sense.

9 Wash Day

Charlene looked at the mountain of laundry in the laundry room and shook her head. Ben had mentioned that towels and sheets were getting scarce and the pile was just too frustrating to look at. The new washer was still untested. She looked at the pile and considered her options. She could load it all in the car and ask Ben for money and go to the laundromat, or simply attack the pile with the new washer and the questionable dryer. Either option would be a two-day task. First she checked for supplies. There was an open twenty-five-pound box of Tide, two gallons of fabric softener, and a case of Clorox. She walked over to the box of Tide and picked it up. There was about five pounds left. That would do today. She would need to go to town to buy some more tomorrow. She checked the dryer. There was a load in it from when the washing machine died. That had to be months ago. It was clean and dry, so she took it out and put it in a basket. It was mostly towels. She put the basket by the door and started sorting laundry. There was one load of dedicates. Those were from her stay in the house. Some of them were hers and some of them were Miranda's. She remembered wearing most of them. That was why she decided to attack the laundry in the first place. There were three loads of coloreds. Some of them had been there since before Christmas, and the rest had accumulated since then. Benny had been trying to handle the whites, and never washed any coloreds before the washer died. Some of the clothes on the bottom of the pile were starting to get moldy. They would need extra treatment. The rest was whites. Sheets pillow cases, towels dish cloths, dish towels, and underwear. That pile was five feet high and twelve feet wide. She started the load of delicates and went upstairs for something to read while the clothes were being washed. She had walked by the study every day, but really didn't have any reason to go in there. She saw floor to ceiling bookshelves as she walked by, but she said well, someday. It was raining outside, and the laundry needed to be done. Today was as close to someday as one could wish. She walked into the study. She stood in the middle of the room and became catatonic from the choices available. Except for a window on the outside wall, and the doorway into the hall, every wall was books. They all looked like somebody had read them. They weren't there for decoration. None of them were sorted into any coherent order except that the children's books, and there were a lot of them, were shelved close to the floor. Up above a child's reach the books were randomly placed. There was Ernest Hemingway's *Farewell to Arms* beside *Babbitt,* beside The *Innocents abroad.* After fingering along about thirty feet of bookshelf, she chose *I the Jury.* She smiled as she thought about what Marjorie would say about that choice. A nice gritty dark detective classic would be nice on a rainy day. It was also the only one by Mickey Spillane that she hadn't read. When she got back to the laundry room, the load of delicates had finished the last rinse and was starting the final spin. When they were finished, she put them in a basket and started a load of towels. While the towels were being washed, she hung the delicates on a clothes line in the other side of the basement. It was a huge room, but it only housed the furnace/ central air conditioning unit and a clothes line. All the maintenance lights were on. Because she spent most of her daylight hours outside, she never noticed that the air conditioning wasn't working. The house was cool enough for her. She thought about Ben. He had mentioned the inoperable system in passing. Nobody called for repairs. Her parents in Connecticut had a similar system. Any two fault lights would shut down the system. After reset without correcting the problem, the next one would shut down the system until someone corrected at least two faults, unless one of the sections that had a fault wasn't needed for the present season. There were four fault lights. All four were on.

"I wish Marjorie were here to see me right now", she muttered under her breath, as she shut off the master switch for the system. The first light was the filter. It was actually two filters the upstream filter was a plain old furnace filter. The second was a hepa-filter made of high density micro fiber. The primary was blocked solid with dust and other household debris. It was sucked into the intake and had places where it no longer made contact with its mounting. It broke when she pulled it out. That was why the hepa-filter plugged. It was solid too. While she was working on the grounds, she got familiar with the contents of the garage. She went to a shelf in the garage and got a filter. The hepa-filter was reusable. She knocked the loose stuff off it and took it into the laundry room to wash it out. The water was black and soupy when she was done. She put the filters back in and went on to the second light. That was the humidifier. The light triggered any time the tank ran dry or the drum failed to rotate. The tank was dry. The drum was white with calcium. The water inlet had a stalactite emerging from it. The water fill float was stuck in the up position. There was a thick layer of calcium on everything.   The   washer finished its final spin and stopped. She took the towels out of the washer and put them in the dryer, loaded a load of tee shirts and boxer shorts in the washer and turned both machines on. There were still at least two more loads of towels. She found the clothes pins and went back into the basement and addressed the humidifier. When she flexed the belt after wrestling it out of the humidifier, it broke in two. She moved on to the dehumidifier. The catch tank was half full of foul smelling liquid. There was a calcium mark from the top of the water level to the full mark on the tank. The full water float was stuck in the full position with calcium residue. She opened the access panel into the plenum and saw a real mess. The line on the humidifier had cracked and sprayed water into the plenum until the calcium plugged the crack. That was where the calcium in the dehumidifier came from. The refrigeration coils of the dehumidifier were coated in calcium as well. She heard the washer stop, so she went back into the laundry room and pulled the load out of the dryer and refilled the dryer and the washer with towels. She folded the first load from the dryer and went back to the furnace/ air conditioner. She opened the access panel for the control circuits and looked at the wiring diagram. It was possible to disconnect the dehumidifier and the humidifier and run the heat and air conditioning function. She went into the garage again and found a screwdriver and disconnected the two damaged sections. She turned the power on and pushed the reset button. The system hummed to life. The delicates were dry so she took them down and folded them into a basket. Before she was finished folding, the washer stopped again. The dryer was still running, so she put the damp towels into a basket and loaded the last load of towels. She made a rough nest in the sheets and sat down to read. The pile of bedding was much more comfortable than the straight backed wooden chair against the wall. Mickey Spillane's rough-hewn prose blended in with the slightly mildewed air of the laundry room. She got into chapter three when the dryer stopped. She pulled out the load of towels and put the towels from the basket in the dryer. The rain outside got louder. And the wind picked up, making the garage doors rattle. She emptied the lint trap and restarted the dryer. She was toward the end of folding the first two loads of towels when the washer finished its load. She had all three baskets in the laundry room full. She found it hard to believe that a house as big and imposing and full as this one would only have three laundry baskets. There had to be more. In the meantime, she took the basket of delicates upstairs to the guest room she occupied and emptied it on the bed. The house was noticeably cooler. The quick fix on the state of the art whole house air conditioning system worked. The air was damp, but it was really damp outside as the rain pelted the house. She made a mental note to herself to talk to Ben about getting a service man over to replace the humidifier and fixing the dehumidifier. She also decided to look for a water softener in the water system. There had to be one. If there was one, it was in dire need of servicing. But now, she had clean underwear. That was the original idea behind the mission. She couldn't remember the last time she showered, or put on the faded black sweat suit that she was wearing. It was bought when she was a freshman at Quinnipiac, a long time ago. It was now filthy from her ad-hoc repair of the heating system. As she passed the mirror, she stopped to take a look at herself. It had been a whole year since the second incident in the park. She had been here for ten months. It seemed like a couple of weeks. Her hair was piled on top of her head in an insane imitation of the Gibson girl look of the late Victorian era. Wisps hung down from it like stray spider webs, and the sun had done it no favors. The color ranged from yellow to dark auburn, depending on position and sun exposure. Anywhere the sun hit her skin was bright red, fading into orange freckles. Looking naked in the mirror, she realized that middle age was knocking on her front door. Her perfect 33C breasts had a bit of a sag to them now because of not wearing support while she worked outside. Her abs were solid and textured. Her knees were bright red and dry with scars from occasionally kneeling on thorns while weeding. Her feet were permanently stained from working barefoot outside and thickly callused. She looked at her hands. Her nails were dirty and broken. As she stepped into the shower, and soaped herself up, she realized that she had never felt better in her entire life. Since the visit to Sid in Jail, she hadn't had a nightmare. When she did remember dreams, they were of sun sand and sea, beautiful men and women and children playing in the Rhode Island surf. She was wearing a bikini and enjoying the attention she attracted. How did it happen, this transformation from a gorgeous young woman to a middle-aged spinster with few prospects? Why did she feel so good? Then she realized that she hadn't brought any towels upstairs.

10 Sermon

Father Bob finished Reading the Gospel and started his homily

"We are a small congregation in a tired old building. Even the veteran's organization didn't want it. The Grange was glad to be out from under it. It's an ugly old building, and we are just ordinary people who nobody really notices, even though they talk to us every day. We are the Church. Not the group of people in Rome and not the building we occupy. It is us! You and me. Our church is you and me doing this thing called a ministry. Jesus told us what that ministry is. It is the same ministry that He and His disciples did two thousand and some years ago. We are here because somehow we were all called upon to service this ministry, and show not just by words and showing up at a particular place at a particular time, but showing by example the teachings of our Savior. He gave us tools for this ministry. He gave us uncountable, endless love .and the most amazingly powerful tool, forgiveness. By experiencing His love for us, we learn to use that love, and forgiveness to teach people that the life is only truly enjoyed if it is shared. Sitting alone up on a mountaintop and not interacting with people is not what He taught. He only went into the wilderness for forty days. He came back from the wilderness and interacted with people. He didn't choose the rich and powerful. He chose ordinary people like us to share his wisdom and love. He loves us enough to give us oneness with Him through the Eucharist. If you are open to it and accept it, you can feel the Holy Spirit entering the deepest recesses of your being. His followers were hunted down and killed for following His Example. The persecution of Christians still goes on today. As was in the days of the Temple, some of the persecution is done by those in the religious organizations. The Sanhedrin were threatened by the ministry, because it threatened their status and position. If the individuals did the charitable works as needed and seen, the organization would not be necessary. The Temple was just a building with a set of traditions attached to it. It was a meeting place where the relationship between Man and Deity was discussed. Like all other big organizations, its bylaws were subtly twisted to give advantage to those at the top of the organization. They perverted the organization to serve them, not God. We must be ever vigilant to make sure that we serve God more than an organization. Our mission is to do for our brethren as we would like them to do for us, even the least of us. Not the beautiful and clever, because they're too self-absorbed to notice or care. Not the rich or powerful, because they are closed to change, but the sick, the outcast, and the downtrodden. We are called to follow in His footsteps, comforting the afflicted ministering to the sick and brokenhearted and forgiving sins. These are our duties as followers of the Lord. It's not about the clergy, but everyone who is practicing the Faith. If we see a wrong, we need to do something about it. Faith without good works is empty. We are the hands of God. We are His angels. Our collective prayers make miracles happen. Prayers with faith and belief along with positive action alter the fabric of the universe. That is how prayer works. Prayer is nothing without belief. Without belief, they are empty words best unspoken. Belief is certain knowledge that the thing you are praying for is within God's will. God always answers our prayers. If you watch and listen He talks to you. He may not say what it is you want to hear, or He might do something entirely different than what it is that you want, but He always answers our prayers. Remember, God sees everything. His Will and desires may be totally different than yours. Sometimes a hardship exists to be nothing but a teachable moment in our lives. We have to be open to the lesson that we have to learn. God made us all. He isn't on anybody's side. When there are sides involved, usually both sides are against the Will of God. Do we do enough to love our enemies? Do we visit the confined? Do we tend to the sick? Do we feed the hungry? Do we comfort those in pain, be it physical or emotional? Are you strong enough to be as a small child and follow our Lord, sometimes at the expense of our lives? This is what each of us is called to do as Christians. If we are strong enough we are truly believing, and the Spirit of the Lord will live within us. We have to look and listen carefully and we can see God's will laid out in front of us. All we have to do is keep in our minds what our mission as Christian people actually is. If it doesn't serve God's will, you will know. The Devil gives us shortcuts. God's path is narrow, twisting and arduous. The difficulty keeps us attentive and awake. Nowhere in any scripture is it ever said that it will be easy. Without difficulty and hardship there would be no growth or knowledge. An easy life makes us weak and soft and complacent. We need to be on our toes and alert to see the wonder of His Creation. We need to be able to notice the little daily miracles before us, like a small child does. We can't let our emotions blind us to them. Mary and Mary Magdalene saw the empty tomb, but thought the worst. When the other disciples saw it they understood, even though they all saw the same thing. Only after they all got together in the upper room did they all understand that death had been conquered. After that, they gladly faced death and persecution to spread the good news. We have to do it by example as well as word. We can't talk the talk without walking the walk. We spread the good news by our actions. Our actions will lead people to hear what we say. What we say must be the truth. We must speak that truth in ways that people understand. We must also understand the truth we are speaking. We must be open to the Holy Spirit so He can show us the way and the Truth. Our every action must reflect that Truth. We all stumble and fall along the way. All of us fall into sin and error. The flesh is weak. When we fall, we must pick ourselves up again, seek forgiveness for any harm we have done, and try again. The Lord is infinite in mercy and forgiveness. Like Him, we should be infinite in our forgiveness too. We are all made of the same stuff as everybody else. We all stumble and fall. As Jesus forgave those who were nailing Him to the cross, we should forgive our brethren for the things that they do. As God loves us, we should love one another. Are you strong enough to do that?

"

11 Maternity Shopping

Main Street in Sterling Forks was only three blocks set in the bottom of a hollow. To the south there was a park. To the north was the fuller's earth processing and packaging plant. To the east was the college and to the west was the suburbs and Interstate 65. The college sprung up around the old Sterling Plantation house, which still served as the administration building and library. When the Sterlings carved the plantation out of the forest, they had ambition and old money. The plantation worked at growing cotton for ten years, but spent all the old money and ambition in doing so. The hard-yellow clay just wouldn't grow cotton. Eventually a bank in Raleigh foreclosed on the property, and sent the Sterlings back up North. A town had already sprung up just west of the plantation, because there was an easy passage through the foothills north to south through the hollow. The old inn and the post office/ general store still stand today. The inn is now a boarding house and the post office/general store is now a post office / 7/11. The town hall is next door to it and is the only non-multipurpose building besides the old inn and the post office/ 7/11. Every other storefront on Main Street had apartments upstairs, accessible from the rear. Iggy Cohen's Woman's Wear was one such building. The Cohens lived upstairs from the store. Sol Schulman lived in the boarding house and had been living there since after his divorce. He was Iggy's sales clerk. Iggy came from Benson Hurst, New York, He came in response to a newspaper ad offering a really good deal on a store with an apartment attached. Iggy was tired of the noise, dirt, and crime in Brooklyn, as well as the high rents in the area. Because he was from Benson Hurst, he never learned to drive. Sol Schulman was his transportation as well as his sales clerk. Until the divorce, Sol lived in the suburbs and commuted back and forth to Lynchburg, and worked as a salesman in a Ford dealership. After the divorce, his alimony payments made the commute impossible. The only reason he still had a car was because Iggy paid his car expenses. Iggy also paid for his breakfast and lunch at the diner. Keeping Kosher in the Bible belt wasn't easy. It wasn't possible at the diner. Earl and Molly were Catholic, and Kenny the cook was Southern Baptist. Because of that, the menu choices for observant Jews left a great deal to be desired. Iggy, Sol, and Fred got a few more or less kosher things added to the menu over the years, but they were Kosher by face value, not ritually Kosher by any stretch of the imagination. Deuteronomy was not a commonly studied section of the Bible in either the Catholic or Southern Baptist churches. The "Kosher" entrees were popular with tourists, travelers and college students, and were in a place of honor on the menu. The preparation of the "Kosher" dishes wasn't by any stretch of the imagination within the dietary guidelines described in Leviticus and Deuteronomy. Diner kitchens are by their very nature not Kosher adaptable. There is just no room.

During lulls in sales in the store, Iggy and Sol discussed the implications of their necessarily sinful ways. As strangers in a strange land, they were excused from a lot of the minutiae of keeping Kosher outside the home. Because Sol lived in the boarding house, he was by ritual law homeless, and excused from a lot more than Iggy. There was a lot of good natured banter about Sol's situation. Living in the Bible belt had a great deal to do with Sol's divorce. It also was the prime cause of the punitive settlement that the judge handed down. All of the ritual holidays were celebrated in Iggy's living room. The Torah was a green bound hard cover book, bought in a bookstore in Nashville. To raise a Minyan to worship meant posting a notice on the college bulletin boards. Other than that, life was good. The store had things that weren't found in Wal-Mart. Everything they sold could be tailored to fit. The idea of two men running a dress shop was the source of a great deal of humor among the townspeople. Iggy's wife running the changing rooms kept the clientele happy, but the jokes still circulated. The women still came to shop and buy the latest New York fashions from size two to size ten. Most of the other offerings went to size 24W. Iggy could match Lane Bryant on both selection and price. He still had many friends in the garment district. He sold a lot of custom plus sizes. He was also the only thing close to a bridal shop in five counties.

Maryanne's clothes were starting to get tight in the middle. She was a regular at the store, so she decided to look for some maternity clothes. Cohen's was the only store in walking distance, so that was the first place she looked. She took Tuesdays and Wednesdays off at the diner because. Those were the slowest days at the diner. Sol was unpacking a box of dresses and hanging them on the rack. Sol's knowledge of woman's wear was sharply limited as he had only been working there for a couple of years

Covenant Roman Catholic Church

and he hadn't paid any attention to it before. It didn't matter as he was a consummate salesman. Maryanne liked and trusted his instincts because he was from Philadelphia and she was from the hills, except the brief time at modeling school in New York City. She didn't see much of the city because after an hour she was terrified to go outside again. It was just too big and too loud and nobody could understand a word she was saying.

"Whatch'all got in ternty stuff? "

"What kind of maternity clothes are you looking for?"

"Ah needs sums stuff fer werk fer one."

"Do you want mix or match or slacks or dresses?"

"Ah gots nairn in ternty stuff t'all"

"OK you're looking for basics I guess"

"Yessah, t' baysics!"

"Well, I can't help you with a work uniform. You'll have to approach your supplier about that, but I think I can set you up with everything else."

"Ah lahks dis 'ere dress".

"That is a wrap around. It should last until you deliver the baby. It expands as you do."

"Ah'll tek it!"

12 Secrets Unearthed

The raised area under the altar had been there since the church was built. If Father Bob hadn't tripped while putting his homily on the lectern on the pulpit, he would never would have found the drawer. It was well hidden. It wasn't locked, just well concealed in the woodwork. He pulled it open. It didn't open easily. It was full of dust, except there were rises and falls in the dust, suggesting something underneath. He pulled the drawer out and took it outside. He dumped it out in the flowerbed beside the front door. Two books fell out along with two brass candlesticks and a large unadorned brass cross. The brass was green with corrosion. The books were large and leather bound. On cleaning the dust off, he revealed a strange writing in gold leaf in an alphabet that he'd never seen before. The other book was smaller, but in the same language. He opened the larger volume. The layout was very familiar. He remembered the similar books he had distributed in

Cameroon, in Bantu and Swahili. They used Arabic script, but the layout was pretty much the same. He picked up the other one. It too was laid out in a familiar style, also in the same strange alphabet. In his studies, he had seen his share of alphabets: Greek, Hebrew, Arabic, Cyrillic, and Sanskrit. This alphabet was different. The capital and lesser letters were identical except in size. They had flowing natural curves and the serifs seemed to be an essential part of the meaning of the letters. It was very elegant and obviously, the product of a printing press. It was too even to have been done by hand. It appealed to the missionary in him. The big one was obviously a Bible, and the other one was probably a Missal or a Catechism. They were probably a protestant sect as their cross was simply a cross. The find brought a warm comfort to him as he thought of the effort that went into those two books. The same two books he had used to bring his faith to West Africa, even though Jesuits were operating missions there since the sixteen hundreds. They were in the local language. The alphabet in his two books was Arabic, and the Language was Swahili. He clasped the two books to his chest. He got up slowly and walked to the Altar and gently put them down. He went back outside and picked up the two candlesticks and the cross, and set them on the altar beside the two books. He felt the same warm presence that he did when he heard the Vietnamese woman's confession. It was the same warm presence that he felt when he celebrated Mass in Cameroon. He walked around to the front of the Alter and knelt, crossed himself and said a prayer of thanksgiving.

"Dear Lord, thank you for revealing this mystery to me. I know now that this was a Holy place for hundreds of years before I came here. Help me bear witness to the faith of the people who came here before me, and worshiped You in this place. Continue being a presence here and give me the strength to be worthy of it. In the name of Jesus, the

Father, Son, and Holy Spirit Amen."

He had been in this church for almost two years, and he still didn't have any adornments for his altar. He had his Paten and Cup for visiting the sick and home bound. They had been with him since his days in West Africa. Now he had candle sticks and a cross. They were obviously blessed and had been used to celebrate the Good News. His congregation didn't have the budget to buy things like that,. so he put the altar decorations in the appropriate places on his Altar. The appearance of great age in their patina gave them an even more reverent air than if they were polished. He left them as he found them, except that he dusted them. He picked up the two books and went back to his quarters. On his way home, he decided to take them over to the college to ascertain the age and origin of them, and what obviously Christian group occupied the church. He was particularly curious about the smaller of the two books. Having been a missionary, he knew what a

Bible looked like in any language. The next morning Father Bob took the smaller of the two books to the college to find out more about it. He started with the foreign language department. The receptionist looked at the book and shook her head. She had never seen that particular language before. The letters were totally unfamiliar to her. She paged the department head. He looked at the type and paged through the book, but couldn't offer anything more than the receptionist did.

"Where did you find this book?"

"Under the altar in my church."

"What church would this be?"

"The old Covenant church over on Oak Street."

Covenant Roman Catholic Church

"There are all kinds of stories about that church. Everyone there disappeared without a trace sometime in the 1830's. It was empty until the Grange took it over in the 1880's. They didn't do much except take out the pews and put a new roof on it. They donated the bell to the war effort, and abandoned it in the 1950's when they built the new hall."

"Do you have any idea of the nationality of the congregation?"

"Back then, that is before the Sterlings came down from Boston, nobody wrote anything down."

"Was the church being used then?"

"No, it was vacant when the Sterlings came."

"How did it survive being vacant for all those years?"

Covenant Roman Catholic Church

"It was perfect for meetings. People kept it up because it was a good gathering place. Even the Klan used it on occasion during reconstruction. If something needed fixing, it got fixed. Did you know that it is the oldest building in Sterling Forks?"

"How old is it?"

"Somewhere between 1765 and 1820 according to various people. It was empty when the Sterlings set up their plantation in the 1840's."

"Was there any kind of settlement here, then?"

"I couldn't tell you that, but, maybe someone in the history department can. All I know is what I was taught during orientation."

Covenant Roman Catholic Church

As Father Bob walked across the small campus, he reflected on the conversation. There was either a mystery or a cover-up about the original congregation of the church. It was obviously Protestant, as it had a cross instead of a crucifix. Because of its largely secular use in the intervening years there were few clues to go by except for the small book he carried. The local history began with the Sterling family, and it was vague, as they left shortly after they came, leaving only a name to the area, and a few settlers that remained as it was a really nice place to live and the railroad came through to service the bankrupt plantation. The location did make a good water stop on the way south to Birmingham. There were so many questions. Who were these people? What happened to them? Why were there no buildings from the same period nearby? Why did the local history stop with the Sterling family? May be the History department could help, but again, maybe not, as it

was hastily added during the '70s to meet liberal arts
degree standards and probably was only there for
show. One could only hope.

The History department head was a beefy
gentleman of Indian descent. Not Native American,
but the genuine article. Father Bob's suspicion about
window dressing seemed to be confirmed by this
fact. He had a Doctorate in International Law
hanging on his office wall from Columbia
University, and his masters and bachelor's degrees
were from Cornell. They were history degrees, but
the masters was in Classical studies, and the
bachelors was in Education. He recognized the type
face right away.

Covenant Roman Catholic Church

"That's Cherokee", he said after a cursory glance at the book. "The alphabet, actually it is a syllabary was developed by a man named Sequoiah in the late 18th century. Unfortunately, I never learned either the code it represents or the language it describes, so I really can't help you as to the content of the book. I know of one person in the area that reads and writes in it, but he's hard to find sometimes. He's an old truck driver from the area, but nobody knows where he lives. The best place to find him is at the diner. Good luck!"

13 Stirrings

The recurring dream made no sense at all to Maryanne. Everything was obscured by a heavy mist or fog. She really couldn't tell. She could hear people weeping, men cursing and here and there horse noises... and footsteps, lots and lots of footsteps. There was a general aura of pain and sadness in the air. It was cold. She awoke with a start. It was as if she had been hurled into her body from a great distance. Her insides quivered. She still felt cold and damp. The baby inside her kicked and twisted, then stretched, and settled back down. She patted her belly.

"It's Awlraht, young'un, she said to the child within her. "Momma's done had 'nother vision.

The dreams started coming when she was in the shack, in the bed. They were unsettling, not in their content, Thousands of faceless people walking in the cold in the same direction, with men on horses cursing and swearing at them as they walked on and on. They were unsettling in the way they ended with her being hurled violently back into her body. The waking state immediately after the dreams was disoriented and foggy, like the weather in the dreams. She tried sleeping in the rocker, but the shock of violent awakening sent the chair over backwards. She was afraid for her baby. At night, the awakenings woke Jack. He would hold her close and reassure her that he would always be there. Jack couldn't always be there. She would be overwhelmed by sleepiness in the middle of the afternoon at work. Molly set up a cot for her in her office. Maryanne gave up the cot after two landings, one which upset the cot. When it happened at home, she would do the ritual that Jack taught her, and sleep on the moss between the rocks. She felt safe there. The landings were just as rough, but at least there was no danger of falling from a piece of furniture. During the dreams, she didn't feel her baby inside her. After the dreams, the baby became very active. She would talk quietly to the baby and caress her belly, hoping that the life inside her was feeling better. At work, life with a baby on board was pleasant. People fussed over her belly like she was family. The tip jar was fuller than it had ever been, and Maryanne was being a full-time waitress. In the middle of the day, she would disappear into the office for about twenty minutes, and except a little shakiness in her hands and voice, finish the day and walk home. People would offer her rides, but she cheerfully refused and said," Ah druther walk, Cain't be gittin all fayat thayah. 'Sides, 'tsgood fer th' young'un."

As she walked through the woods, she'd sing at the top of her lungs. She would sing the old hymns her daddy taught her, or current country songs from the jukebox in the diner. Sometimes, she would let the forest sing to her. The forest to her was a gleeful thousand voice choir, singing in an ancient language understood by her soul. That was the song she loved best. The baby loved it too. She could feel the happiness inside her. The dreams were distant then. Sleep was distant too. Night time was her favorite time to walk home. She could see the stars through breaks in the canopy above her. There weren't as many as she remembered seeing when she was very little, up in the Rocky Top. They weren't as bright either. She loved looking at them anyway and talking to her small internal passenger about them. In the background, crept sleep with the dream inside it. She couldn't put her finger on what bothered her about the dream. Was it the stress she felt when she was dreaming? Was it the feeling of confinement and the darkness of her surroundings? Was it the voices outside, some in the language from the rocks, and some in English? The English was loud and abusive. The language from the rocks was submissive and pained. She put it aside as she turned onto the mossy path into the woods toward the shack. The soft moss caressed her bare feet as

Covenant Roman Catholic Church

she walked the last mile home.

Jack had a venison stew ready for her when she walked in the door. The aroma of ramps and wild fennel filled the cozy little shack. There was corn bread and wild mustard greens to compliment the stew. As usual very little on the table came from the grocery store. It either came from the forest or the small garden patch in the clearing. As usual it was tasty and nutritious. As they ate, they caught up on each other's day. Maryanne brought news from town. Mostly it was the usual small town gossip. The diner was a great source for it.

"Fathah Bob ovah to the cov'nant church found two old books undah th' altah."

"Oh?"

"Yeah, They wuz in some strange writin whut he'd ne'er seed befah."

"Old y' say, how old?"

"Real old, dusty too!"

Covenant Roman Catholic Church

"Whud dey look like?"

"He sed one, he wuz purty sure wuz a Bible, but he'd no ken whut t'other one wuz"

"Did he say whut th' writin looked like?"

"Yeah, kinda curvy with ears 'n points 'n tails 'n stuff."

"Well, I guess we got 'nother reason to go see Pop."

"When we gonna do that?"

"Soon, ah hopes."

Y' git th' deer inta th' smokehouse?

"Yep! Smokehouse's full now!"

"Guess ah gotta scrape th' hide t'nite."

"'T's all stretched."

Covenant Roman Catholic Church

14 Service call

The man from Huntsville Environmental services spent the better part of a day in the basement of Benny's house. There was heavy corrosion damage in the plenum of the system. The humidifier and dehumidifier were a total loss. The corrosion almost compromised the evaporator housing. A lot of rust had to be vacuumed out of the fins. Even the sensors had to be replaced. Charlene brought him sweet tea and watched him as he worked, asking questions along the way. It was too big a job for her to deal with on her own, but she wanted to know how to do it if it happened again, or better yet how to prevent a recurrence.

"How long do you think that thing has been leaking before it caused the dehumidifier to fail?"

"Looks like about a year or so."

"What's that white stuff all over everything in there?"

"Lime."

Covenant Roman Catholic Church

"From the water?"

"Yep! We're sitting on a huge block of limestone. All the ground water around these parts flows over, under, around, and through it."

"If it left white stuff in here, why is the stuff I scrub from around the drains reddish brown?"

"A lot of the pipes in the water system are iron. The lime makes the water slightly alkaline, so it picks up iron from the pipes. As it evaporates it leaves iron behind. This leak was big enough for a long enough period, that there was more lime than iron left behind. It you took this stuff to a lab, you would find iron too."

"I can't help but notice that you are replacing all the copper pipes with plastic here. Wouldn't copper like what was there be better?"

"No. This plastic will be more reliable. The copper corroded through after about twenty years. This plastic with stainless fittings won't ever corrode. Not only that, if the house is left unattended, and there is a hard freeze, it won't rupture."

"Yeah, I remember having to replace a lot of pipes after the big ice storm in Connecticut. It cost Dad's insurance company a fortune. We had to take walls out. Dad bought a generator after that one. We were in a motel for three weeks. The power was only off for a few days."

"It doesn't get that bad here, but if there is a regulator failure in this system, the refrigeration section in this system will freeze the pipes that are inside the plenum. It's better to do the whole thing in this plastic stuff."

During the interaction with the repairman, Charlene noticed something unsettling. He wasn't giving her any sort of special attention. Usually younger men, even some middle-aged men had trouble concentrating around her, and had trouble carrying on a conversation. They stared. This guy didn't. He was friendly and businesslike, even with the two of them alone in the basement. Not only that, but she was relaxed around him. She wasn't sure which was more unsettling. She enjoyed watching him work. It was almost magical to see three sheets of galvanized steel turn into a plenum and all the necessary gussets and flaps needed to control the airflow through it. It was a delight to see and hear the system purr back to life with no malfunction lights on. She felt drawn to him as he leaned against the washing machine as he filled out the invoice. She didn't expect that at all. It had been such a long time since she'd had that feeling, that it totally surprised her. She blushed and stammered when he handed her the paper. She was really glad that she didn't own the house when she saw the numbers, but she hoped that the repairman didn't notice what was going on inside her.

15 Unole's Birth

It was hot. The leaves drooped on the trees. The birds and insects were too hot to say much to each other. Just a kind of halfhearted chirping to ritually mark territory, but not much else. The air was hard to breathe. Even in the shade, there were no cool spots...except two. One was the spring house. It wasn't inhabitable because the ceiling was low, and the spiders only left enough room to dip a bucket. The other was the space between the twin rocks. It was always shady there and the monoliths absorbed a huge amount of cold during the winter, so they heated very slowly. They also were more or less surrounded by large trees. Between the rocks was inviting. She felt the comfort therein calling her. Her clothes clung to every inch of her body. Water dripped off the hem of her wrap around maternity dress. The child inside her was displaying discomfort too by elbowing the landscape. Maryanne felt huge and sluggish. Since the heat started it was hard to eat. Her stomach was always upset. She snapped at Jack that morning over nothing. She never remembered being so uncomfortable. Heat rash covered most of her body, and her clothing aggravated the situation by being wet and sticky, and not moving when she did, aggravating the heat rash. She was the most miserable she ever remembered being. The shack provided shade to an extent, but the ancient wood and stone didn't do anything to keep out the heat. It was time to find a cooler place. She had been having pangs in her lower abdomen for the last two or three days. Some of them were a minor distraction, and others stopped her in her tracks until they passed. Jack was in the woods checking on his bees. Hot days were good to work with them because they would be mostly out foraging and the combs would be lightly defended. She was alone in the shack when another pang hit. It knocked her to her knees and made her dizzy. The baby inside her squirmed and kicked as well. That and the heat sealed the deal. She would fill the water jug and move in between the rocks, until it got cooler. She scrawled a quick note to Jack and set out for the rocks. She had to stop in the big clearing for another contraction, which was worse than the last. She sat on one of the logs around the fire pit until it passed. She waddled the rest of the way to the rocks, only stopping a couple of times to drink from the jug. As she crawled through the opening into the hollow, she felt really nauseous. The only thing that came up was the last drink of water. She collapsed in a contraction onto the soft cool moss, where she spent so many hot afternoons. It felt so good to be there. The contractions were getting closer together, and a lot stronger. She felt safe and secure though. The voices from the rocks comforted her. When Jack told her about the voices, she laughed, "How can them big ole rawks tawk", she laughed. She wasn't laughing now. The voices, mostly female, now, said comforting things, reassuring things. She was totally alone, but the voices were company and help. As she tuned her mind into the voices, the pain from the contractions lessened. The voices blended together into an ancient song. Thunder rumbled in the distance. The voices chanted and sang about the beginnings and sometimes endings of life.

We are pushed

Out into the world

And in turn

We push out

Our sons and daughters

Into the world

As our mothers

Did before

Covenant Roman Catholic Church

And our daughters

Will do in

The future

The Mother

Has made us mothers

To share

In the act of creation

As our mothers

Shared with us

We share it

With our daughters

The mother

Gave us a gift

To us

Covenant Roman Catholic Church

And us alone

As we are mothers too

The act of creation

Is our gift

To us

And the world

We give the gift

We are the gift

Without us

There is no one

There is no greater gift

Than the life

From our wombs

Hearken my child

It is hard work

Covenant Roman Catholic Church

Your heart must be strong

Your heart must be pure

During this time

You are

The mother

The Mother of us all

Through your loins

Passes the universe

Everything known

Everything felt

Everything loved

Peace be on you

Child of the mother

Mother of the child

Covenant Roman Catholic Church

The future of us all

Fear not

For even in death

There is life

And in life

Death

As it is

As it always was

And as it should be

A renewal

Of body

Of soul

Of spirit.

Pain can be pleasure

If it brings beauty

Covenant Roman Catholic Church

As pleasure can be pain

If it brings ruin

Mind these things

In the act of becoming

In the act of creating

Together as one

Then as two

There was another rumble, louder and closer. Her water broke. It flowed over her thighs into the moss, and disappeared. There was another huge contraction that stopped her breath and brought tears to her eyes. The thunder rumbled again, louder than before. The air took on a heavy quality and it got darker in the hollow between the rocks. The voices became gentler, more loving and soothing as they continued:

We are here for you

We have done

What you are doing

And your daughters

Will do

In the future

As you will be there for them

Listen to us

Do as we say

You are the Mother now

The Mother of us all

Thunder rumbled even louder this time followed by the sound of wind moving in the trees outside. Another stronger contraction swept through her body. She felt a pulling in her pelvic floor. The child inside her kicked and punched. The voice from the dreams said, "It's time", followed by another kick from inside. The voices stopped singing. A mature female voice said, "Maryanne, listen! I will tell you what to do. Focus on me, and there will be no pain." A stronger wind moved through the trees outside. The mighty trees that had been there since the days of Sequoyah moaned as their branches moved in the wind. A cooling breeze came through the small opening. Maryann took off the wraparound dress and put it aside. It was totally soaked. She took off her shirt, actually one of Jacks tee shirts and wrung it out. Another gust of wind moved the trees outside. A flash of lightning lit up the little haven followed immediately by a very loud thunderclap. Yet another big contraction. The tightness in her pelvic floor got stronger. The child kicked again. The voice from the dream said "I want out now!" The mature female voice said, "Put your back against the rock behind you and squat with your feet apart as far as you can". She complied. It was hard because another contraction interrupted the move. It was strong enough to gray out her vision. She panted from the exertion. As she moved into the squat, the tightness eased in her pelvic floor. The kick from inside became a steady push. The voice outside said, "wait for the peak of the next contraction." Outside the wind became a steady roar increasing in intensity. Another strong contraction swept through her. She waited as she was told. It was hard to wait, as she had an impulse to push. The contraction intensified as did the roar outside. She could hear things snapping and breaking outside. The voice said, "Push, Now, Hard!" She felt a tearing as she pushed. Her child pushed too. The air became very still and very light. The noise outside was deafening. The snapping and cracking became scraping and breaking. Things were crashing against the rocks. The voice said, "Harder! Push!" She pushed. Her vision grayed out again as she pushed. She could feel the child inside pushing too. She could feel more tearing in her pelvic floor and the child moving toward the outside. The contraction stopped. She stopped pushing and waited for another. The voices started singing again. The words were foreign but triumphant in tone. It was obviously a song of joy. Another contraction came.

She pushed. The child moved more to the outside, faster than before. She felt something against her thigh. She pushed harder. Suddenly the noise outside stopped. There was a rush from inside her and there was a baby on the moss underneath her. She pushed again involuntarily and the placenta followed. She lay back against the stone and panted she was suddenly filled with peace and clarity. She tore a strip from the bottom of the tee shirt and tied off the umbilical cord then she bit through it, separating it from the placenta. She then lay back and put the baby to her breast. It was a girl, with red hair. She wiped the blood and mucus from her and wrapped her in the tee shirt. They were mother and daughter. The voices fell silent. It was raining outside. Between the rocks it was quiet, dry and secure. She looked at her daughter and said to her, "I am going to call you Lucille." The voice from the dreams said "OK but, my name is Unole Adeloho's'gi. I will allow you to call me Lucille, but

nobody else! I am Adeloho's'gi! Unole because of the cyclone, but Adeloho's'gi for my life and role."
Then her voice fell silent, and the baby cried. They sat together and rested in the space between the rocks. Outside, the hilltop was scoured clean of vegetation. Even the thin soil was gone.

16 Book Sales

Fred's new book had been out for eight months before it got a review. It was from an independent newspaper from Chicago. It was a four-star review by the in house literary critic.

"Fred Katz's *Making of a Misogynist* is a cautionary tale about what happens when a person becomes too absorbed in any one thing. It also is a life lesson we should all heed about not getting involved with others in outside activities. In short, living a superficial life can and will be hazardous to your health." The clipping came from his agent folded into a resignation letter. The letter said:

"Fred,

It pains me to write this letter. We have been together for ten years. The last three have given me gray hairs. Keeping your publisher interested in your second book took a superhuman effort. They wanted to dump you more than once on the project for lack of progress. The book they published was to fill a contract, not to make an effort to promote. They weren't happy with the finished product because it didn't target the same market your first book did. They want out of the contract on both books, because maintaining a stable is no longer profitable. They ran off a print run to satisfy the contract and dumped it in Chicago. They also canceled a sixth printing on the first. I live off royalties. No sales, no royalties. I liked the book, but me, and a few readers in Chicago don't generate royalties. I send my regrets.

Sam."

Fred read the letter and the clipping. He was stunned. He didn't expect anything like that as a reaction to his book. It was the best thing he had ever written. It was the most meaningful thing he had done in his life, but he was abandoned by both his publisher and his agent because of it. He felt sick to his stomach. The clipping made it worse. With proper promotion, it could have had modest sales, and he could have been back on the steel breeze of promotion. Now he would miss all that, and in the process, need to find a new agent. Losing his agent and his publisher, as well as the rights to two books was a total tragedy. The scope of it was still unmeasurable, as until a few minutes ago, he was blissfully unaware of it. He stood in the doorway in stunned silence. No new royalties, no income, a single check of an unknown amount for the wholesaled books, God only knows when, and nothing in the pipeline. "Way to hit bottom, Fred" he muttered to himself as he walked to the kitchen. He put the letter and the clipping on the table and sat down to reflect on the new situation. He was a published author with a best seller under his belt. That might get the teaching position back, if the college wanted to spend the money. His little adventure with food poisoning and being kidnaped caused the loss of that job. He probably would have to grovel and beg as creative writing teachers with B.A.s are a dime a dozen. Mail order editing? Where does one get the work? Magazine work? Full compost file already with magazine work. File cabinet full of rejection letters. Actual work experience: none. Occupation, writer/ author, never having done anything else, except teaching sophomore creative writing at a small liberal arts college. He jotted his ideas on a yellow legal pad. The page filled fast. Every idea had several reasons for not being applicable. Four pages in, he got up and looked for beer. As usual, there wasn't any. Not only that, but the letter came instead of the expected royalty check. The last one was a four-digit number with a decimal point in the middle. He really needed that second book. They were all except a few in a discount book warehouse destined for Dollar Stores and bodegas, with no chance for a second printing. When it suited the lawyers, he would get a check with promotion expenses and the advance deducted

from it- when it suited the lawyers. Party over Fred!
Sin loi GI! Worse yet, Marjorie didn't know a thing.
Marjorie had given up her profitable scam and was
working for Visiting Nurses. Not driving was a huge
handicap for her, as she was dependent on the local
bus system that was geared to college students, or
shoe leather express. Fred had also given up driving,
as supporting a car was more money than he wanted
to spend. It had been years since he renewed his
license, so he would have to start from scratch, and
being from down town Philadelphia, he never drove
much anyway. He was never comfortable behind the
wheel. He continued to scribble his alternatives on
the legal pad. Every alternative has at least three
reasons why it wasn't possible. Sharing quarters
with Marjorie, for example. She still had the little
two room behind the school clinic. She also had a
paid motel room anywhere there was a Best
Western. The idea of living in a motel since his
kidnapping/ forced vacation gave him the willies. It

wasn't just the motel room but Marjorie as well. He loved her, but... She had kept him comatose for two months and still hadn't said much about that time period. She had used the same methods to cut a man to total incontinence, making sure that he survived to experience it. She was still very wary of showing affection to anyone, real closeness seemed impossible, even after almost a year of seeing each other. Emotionally, she was an enigma. She could laugh and joke around, but still seemed distant. He wasn't sure she was capable of real long term love, the kind he craved desperately. In short, she scared him as much as motel rooms. Worse yet, he was financially dependent on her now, as he had borrowed money from her to make rent, over the last couple of months while the book wound its way through the marketing channels. She was willing, because she had read and enjoyed both opuses. Now the marketing channels had come to a sudden spiteful dead end in a warehouse somewhere in

Chicago. He knew the depths of her anger. He had seen it. How could he tell her what happened to him without either being killed or nullified? As he puzzled, he scribbled notes on the legal pad. The seeds of a novel sprung out at him. The subject matter was of a sort that were beyond pornography. He scribbled wildly as images spun through his brain. Marjorie's unique experiences would be a treasure trove for research, if he could get her to open up. In the meantime, he had to start looking for a new publisher. For that he needed a proposal. It needed to go to agents and publishers, to find someone to take on a new but proven client and a very edgy work. He flipped over to another blank page and started writing. Panic turned to thought, and then to determination in a little over three hours.

17 Scared Straight

Sid sat on a folding chair at the end of the medium security visitors' lounge. It was the first time he had ever been there. The last and only visitors he had were in the max visitor's lounge. He had only had two in his entire prison experience. Where the max was dingy, dark and divided, this was a big open clean room. Instead of the institutional green walls, this room was a light flamingo pink. Four rows of folding chairs were set up facing Sid's chair. Sid was dressed in his modified stained orange jumpsuit. He had fasted for two days to keep the leakage down to a minimum. He drank a bottle of Maalox to neutralize the digestive juices that were pooling in his depend. He was nervous. He had never done anything like this before. He wasn't sure he could. The teenagers that were coming were sex offenders from a couple of juvenile units. They were all first offenders from good families. Their families applied to have their children go through this program. It was called scared straight. It was a program that hopefully would impress upon the immature minds of the young offenders the end result of a life of crime. Sid, a lifetime criminal, specializing in sexual offenses, was their instructor. Before he ended up there on the present conviction, those teenagers would have been considered prey for him. Gender was unimportant to him in those days. Release and power were his motivations. He loved generating fear. The sexual release was just a byproduct. Now, he was fearful. He was weak and outnumbered. He also had life in the hole if he screwed up this project. It was the most important thing he had ever done.

Covenant Roman Catholic Church

He heard voices in the corridor. They were young voices. There were boys and girls in the group. He was hoping to have only boys, but someone in Corrections didn't bother to check gender on the applications, so there were four girls in the group. They walked in laughing and joking with each other, nudging and pushing as they chose their seats, totally oblivious of Sid at the head of the room. They giggled and talked until the escorting corrections officer blew his whistle. The murmur died down to a few whispers. The correction officer walked to the head of the room and blew the whistle again. This time he got his desired quiet.

"Ladies and gentlemen, this is Sid. He is in here this time for forty counts of aggravated sexual assault and four counts of forcible rape. He has a record of prior convictions for pandering, sexual assault, sodomy, blackmail and attempted murder. He's been our guest here for twenty-seven years, mostly hard time."   Sid stood up and took a step from the chair. His throat was dry. His hands were shaking. He had never done anything like this in his life, and he could feel it. The depend chafed his crotch as he moved. In spite of the precautions he took to slow down the flow of juices, it was soaked.

"Kids, I am what will happen to you if you keep on your present path. I bounced in and out of juvie for eight years. I was an angry kid. I stole stuff, I beat up people, and took their money. I started getting off on their fear. I was in control. I took whatever was most valuable to them. I discovered that raping people took away the anger for a while. I got off on the fear and the begging. I enjoyed the struggle. The anger always came back. I wanted to hurt people. I always got caught. I did time. I got my fear jollies here too, raping other prisoners. I spent years in the hole. I hated everyone, and everyone hated me. I didn't give a rat's ass. I would play the game here for a couple of years, and they would kick me out. I was never out for more

than a month before I would be in court again, and
then back here. One day I raped a woman who was as
angry as I was. Then I raped her friend, next time I
was out. I got caught on another crime and was inside
for a while. I went back to the same town, because
college students are easy, and they are easy to swindle.
The two women I raped there found me and took their
revenge."

Sid unbuttoned his jumpsuit and let it slide to
the floor. The depend was actively dripping
digestive juices. He popped the tape on the depend
and dropped it to the floor. And stood there with his
feet spread, as the juices dripped from the opening
between his legs. Two of the girls fainted. Several of
the boys vomited violently. Everyone jumped away
from their chairs and moved to the far end of the
room. The biggest of the boys started weeping
uncontrollably. He was a part of a gang rape that
hospitalized the girl involved.

"This is what eventually happens to sex offenders. Look and remember. I was where you are now. I didn't ask for help. My selfish anger brought me here. I caused this. I deserved this. You have time. Whatever it takes, sexual violence does this. Not just to your victim, but to you as well. Somebody somewhere will eventually remember and get even. You are lucky to be in America. There is help here. Use it! Don't be afraid of seeming weak, or what your friends think. It's your ass I'm talking about."

He started walking toward the group. They recoiled in fear and revulsion. The juices were a steady stream down the insides of both his legs.

"Here, reach out and touch the reality of it! This is what happens to sexual predators, if they keep at it long enough."

"OK Sid, you've made your point, I don't think you need to say or do more. Let's go back and get you cleaned up."

"Yeah, I think I've made my point. At least I hope so!"

With that the guard and Sid walked out of the room, leaving the jumpsuit and the depend behind on the floor and a trail out the door. Sid was getting a little light headed, but he felt good. He didn't remember feeling that good for a long long time.

Covenant Roman Catholic Church

18 Unole as an Infant

It would not be exaggeration to say that Unole was not the typical princess. She was brash, loud, argumentative, and stubborn. She shunned any toy that even suggested princess. She was a red-haired streak of lightning tearing through the lives of her family. She supplemented her diet with insects, woodland plants and small animals, eaten raw. Even birds were no match for her lightning hands and silent tread. She would stalk them for hours, inching closer and closer, until they were squirming briefly in her grasp. Then they were gone in two or three bites. This went on from since before she could walk. It was like she was born to hunt.

"Jack, she's a'eatin bugs 'n stuff"

"She gitten sick?"

"No, she's makin me sick watchin her".   "Wha'dya want me to do about it?"   "She's y'all's

127

daughter!"   "If it ain't

hurtin her, I ain't, gonna stop her, even if I could

do it."

"She's eatin bugs!"

"Yeah, I sees it."

"I seed her eat a bird yesterday!"

"Where'd she git a bird?"

"She jumped on it, like a cat!"

The argument over Unole's eating habits

ended in a draw. Unole climbed into Maryanne's

lap and cuddled up and yawned.

"Lord, what am I gonna do with this

girl?" she muttered. Jack laughed and said,

"Love her."

Maryanne was more than a bit

disappointed. Here was the daughter she always

wanted, but the total opposite of what she

dreamed of. More of a son than a daughter.

Maryanne wanted lacy dresses and velvet. Unole

wanted nakedness. They compromised on a

loincloth made from a cloth diaper and a piece

of clothesline. This was because the life

expectancy of a disposable diaper was measured

in seconds. As soon as she developed the

dexterity to remove them, she did. She also

hated being indoors. Initially, Maryanne worried

about Unole getting sunburned, but she tanned

to a beautiful bronze color very quickly. The

other matter was hair. It was curly, it was

tangled, and it was full of foreign objects. She

didn't like having it groomed either, so it was an

orange and brown frizz with sticks and leaves

poking out of it. Occasionally, when the tangles

got painful, Unole would permit her hair to be

shampooed and combed out, but not without a

struggle and considerable tears from both

groomer and groomed. When her hair was

combed out and clean she was a darling little girl

in a white cotton loincloth. She refused to wear

anything else. She was strong enough to enforce

it. Maryanne was at her wits end. The one-sided conversations would be: "Lucille, No!" or "Lucille, little girls don't do that!" or "Lucille, you can't eat that!", or "Lucille! Get over here, now!"   Toilet training was a total nightmare. There was no indoor plumbing in the shack. The outhouse was over a hundred feet away, and any water had to be carried from the spring. On top of that, Unole didn't really care if she was soiled or not, much less wet. If the loincloth got too heavy, it would fall off by itself, so Unole would invariably end up running around outside naked. Because of this, diaper rash was never a problem, but policing up soiled diapers from under the bushes was a constant activity, as they never seemed to fall off in open territory. Maryanne longed for the easy days in the diner. She was also afraid that someone from the diner would show up, with her daughter running around outside filthy and naked, which

was more often than she wanted to admit to
allowing. Heaven forbid that someone would see
her eating bugs and birds. The diapers on the
clothesline were streaked with brown and green
that the ancient Maytag on the porch couldn't
wash out, even with the best of modern
detergents. She felt like a failure as a mother.
Then, Unole would come in, climb up in her lap,
nurse for a while, then curl up and go to sleep in
her lap. The feeling of failure would magically
disappear. This wasn't the little princess in pink
and lace, all soft and fragrant. This was a tough
solid child of the woods that was dirty and
rough. Her knees and elbows were skinned from
crawling in the dirt and rocks in the dooryard
and beyond. Her hair was matted as usual with
sticks and leaves, but she was her daughter, and
she loved her. She also realized that there was
no way that they could live like this in town.
Child welfare would take her out and hang her

for neglect, even though she did her absolute best. The birth certificate said Lucille, a name only her mother could use. She was Unole Adelohos'gi, raised on locusts and wild honey, fearless warrior and child of the storm. The storm that cleansed the Holy Place, where she was born.

19 Father Bob meets Francis

The History department head gave Father Bob very little information about the mysterious truck driver that could be found at the diner, except that he could read and write Sequoian script. To get to the diner, he had to walk clear across town. Like most towns, Sterling forks was bypassed when the interstate went through, as uninhabited land was cheaper than widening existing main streets. The diner was about two miles west of town. The diner was on a service road built to serve the interstate. It wasn't a major truck stop, but it had a garage and a fuel station with heavy duty towing. There was no bus service to it. It brought back memories of his ministry in Cameroon, where everybody walked everywhere. Catching a ride with Molly was a one-way trip, as Molly would go to the diner, and stay for ten or twelve hours at a time, and her hours were whenever she was needed. She also ran an accounting office down town, so the days she was available for transportation to the diner were even fewer, as she would work at the downtown office, and go straight to the diner. His rectory was still a bedroom in Earl and Molly's house. Staking out the diner to meet Francis was a major undertaking. Any way he looked at it, it would take a major amount of time away from his parochial duties. The smaller book weighed upon his mind. He had the stereotypical idea about Native American culture. It didn't jibe at all with a little clapboard Christian church in the middle of nowhere. What were their beliefs? How did they receive the Gospel? What was prayer like for them? He obsessed over it.

Over time, Father Bob thought that Francis was like the Loch Ness monster or Bigfoot, a myth, as everybody knew about him, but nobody could actually document a real sighting...until he met Fred. He met Fred through Marjorie. Marjorie brought him to Mass. Fred also brought a whole new slant to Belief. It was a simple group of words in Hebrew called the Kiddush, the blessing of bread and wine. It would now come to him while celebrating the Eucharist. *Baruch atou Adonai, Elohenu Moloch cholem Boeri parei haga vanu* for *bread,* and *haga fen* for wine. Pretty much what Jesus said when blessing the bread and wine during the Last Supper. It made him feel oneness with the Lord when he blessed the Sacrament. Fred knew Francis, and could introduce them. Even Fred admitted that Francis was hard to catch, as he was semiretired, and only drove runs when his customer needed it done. Fred was almost as hard to catch in the diner as Francis was because Fred too was a pedestrian. Francis was mobile. If Father Bob hadn't met Fred, it would be an impossible task, as he had no idea as to what the mystery man looked like, much less his name. Fred knew him, so it was simply a matter of time and circumstance for the three of them to get together.

It didn't go that way though. Father Bob had walked out to the diner after lunch one Wednesday. He had his bag with him, as he always carried it with him. The small book was in the bag. He took comfort in its being there, as it must have been a very holy book to the people in that church to be hidden under the altar. He ate his lunch at the counter, as he usually did when he was there alone. He made small talk with a few of the regulars, and ate his sandwich. He was on his way out the door, when he felt a touch on his shoulder.

"Hi Padre, I hear that you're looking for me."

Covenant Roman Catholic Church

The touch and the voice startled him. He hadn't seen or heard anyone approaching him. He turned to face a disheveled old man in worn work clothes. He was speechless.

"They say you have a book you want me to look at."

"Book? Book.....book....Oh yes I found this book under the altar of my church. The History Department head said that you could tell me what it is."

He dug into his bag and pulled out the ancient book.

"Ah! A Common Book! The only place I ever saw another one of these was at Trail's End in Oklahoma."

"Common book?"

"Yes, the Common Book of Prayer"

"Like the Presperterian Church?"

"Exactly! It was translated into Cherokee shortly after Sequoyah developed the syllabary. There were over a million printed. It was the second book printed in Cherokee. The Bible was the first. Most of them were confiscated by the government and burned."

"Why would the government want to burn prayer books?"

"To propagate the myth of heathen savages so they could take our land."

"Why didn't anybody say something?"

"America was in love with Andy Jackson, the War Hero President. Besides, most of the soldiers couldn't do much else than sign their names. The books were in Cherokee in Sequoian Script. To them, it was devil writing. They burned most of the Bibles."

"The Cherokee were Presperterian?"

"The largest Prespertary in the country, over two million people. The rest were Baptists. It didn't matter, they got herded to Oklahoma too."

" I never read or heard about it."

"They don't teach it in school. Did you know that until fifteen years ago, it was illegal to speak Cherokee in public?"

"I thought....."

Covenant Roman Catholic Church

"The Native Americans aren't considered Americans, unless they are needed to fight wars. We are considered by the government to be less valuable then wildlife. A deer has more rights than one of us. Yet, every war this nation has fought, the indigenous people have fought and died, as well as provided things that won the war. Did you ever hear of the Wind Talkers during World War Two? They used their language to convey messages so that the Japanese and the Germans couldn't intercept them and use the information. It was a foolproof, unbreakable code that was illegal to use as everyday speech by the people that spoke it every day."

20 Marjorie the Visiting Nurse

To say Visiting Nurses was a misfit career for Marjorie was an understatement. She liked dealing with the patients in their home environments, but... Visiting Nurses assumed that the nurses would have a car and drive. Marjorie walked or took public transit. In a sleepy little college town, mass transit was a joke. It went somewhat into the suburbs, but the schedule was spotty or nonexistent once one passed the incorporated area of Sterling Forks. There was a taxi, if you could call a retired roofer in an old Checker, a taxi company. He went out when he felt like it, and would disappear to Florida for six weeks every winter. The only reason Visiting nurses kept her was her skill in post-surgical treatment. She managed dressings, drains, catheters, and some physical /occupational therapy, with a skill level only found in big cities. She was better in most ways than the local doctor, as she had experience as a surgical nurse in a busy hospital before she came to town to run the front side of the college clinic. She left the clinic suddenly, after being raped and ignored, and disappeared for a couple of years. Because of the abruptness of her departure, they didn't want her back. Now she was working harder for half the money she had made at the clinic. After atoning for her post rape behavior, she gave up her side income and interstate travel to help local citizens through their illnesses and disabilities. Officially, her job was a four hour a day, part time gig. Travel kicked the four hours to twelve. She was tired all the time and sometimes cranky. She liked the solitude at home sometimes, but at others, she missed Charlene. Charlene was moody and withdrawn, but she was there, and there was company at mealtimes. Eating alone sucked. She had a new understanding of Fred's food poisoning episode. She neglected buying groceries, neglected checking the refrigerator and shelves for spoilage, and did dishes only when she couldn't find a clean coffee cup. She needed a change. She thought long and hard about moving in with Fred, but she had never shared living arrangements with a man. She wasn't sure that she wanted to. She wasn't sure she could still stay there and subsidize Fred's rent while waiting for the second book to sell and generate money. She had burned through her savings and was living solely off Visiting Nurses. She needed income. She wasn't afraid to skirt the law, as she had done it to some extent after the rape, when she was too angry to work. She had already repaired a couple of gunshot wounds that the victims wanted kept quiet, and a few knife wounds in similar circumstances. Even in sleepy little college towns there was a certain level of interpersonal violence. She was available, competent, and discrete. There was also a fairly good payoff from those endeavors, but they were sporadic, and inconvenient in timing. The new side business paid better than Visiting Nurses. One gunshot wound was worth three weeks of running after buses and walking suburban streets and roads. With that and her occasional illicit herb sales, she was surviving. This was a side of her life that she didn't want Fred to see. If she moved in with him, he would find out about it. She was not sure how he would handle it. It always freaked out Charlene, when she came home at two AM with blood on her. What would Fred think in a similar circumstance? Besides, she wasn't interested in a sexual relationship yet, if at all. She wasn't sure if Fred was capable of being platonic, because of the two months in the motel, and the fact that he had been married before.   "Why must life be so complicated", she mumbled, as she stood waiting for the cross-town bus. She had a diabetic, and a mental patient left for the day, and it was already late. She had missed lunch, because she had to walk two miles from the bus stop, change a dressing on a burn patient, walk the two miles and catch the bus again. "What was I thinking? There's no way this job can be done properly without driving." She paced back and forth. The bus was late again, or did she miss it? She was never sure. She had been using that bus line for ten years, and she was never sure if she could get anywhere on time. Atlanta was great. It was a metropolitan system with modern equipment and federal subsidies. It was always within a minute or two of being on time. Even Nashville had a somewhat meaningful system. This was a piss ant little college town with a rinky-dink college subsidized bus line, on a par with a rural school bus system in a poor county in Mississippi. "A third world banana republic has better transit", she mused.

21 Urine Race

The stock holders meeting in Atlanta was on Monday. Benny still couldn't get his prosthesis to go in. He could with effort, insert his thumb. He would have to negotiate two airports, a major U S city, and a major business meeting as a female in drag. This included entertaining guests in a hotel room. Coffee and alcohol would also be involved. Ben was terrified. His hair had come in. Strangely, all the gray was gone. His beard only came in sparsely, but it had no gray either. Except for a small weight gain, he looked normal, although ten years younger. As he shaved, he considered himself in the mirror. A lot of the wrinkles, gained over the years of high pressure corporate work were gone. His hair was softer and finer. His eyebrows were subtly different. It would be a three-day meeting, and because of his holdings, he had to be there. They were going to celebrate his retirement... in style. There would be a dinner and the Press would be there. He would be the center of attention. The company was going to recognize his contributions. He had sixteen patents and was responsible for half the source code for the software. Over the years, he had generated almost a billion dollars in sales. Most of the sales were done personally, in meetings in foreign lands. He was a legend there. He also had to exercise certain bodily functions. Urination, whether he wanted to admit it or not, would require pulling down his pants. It was the reason for the prosthesis. He liked the freedom at night from needing to turn on the light to pee. He liked not having to adjust himself to put on his pants. He secretly liked wearing panties. He was wearing them all the time now, as there was no reason to wear boxers anymore. Even tighty whities felt stupid. Miranda had left him hundreds of pairs of white cotton panties, and they fit perfectly. Nobody in the corporation knew the extent of his surgery. He really didn't want to let them know. As he packed for the trip he pondered about the panties. What if someone saw them in the hotel room without the necessary woman to go with them? He had a reputation as a straight married guy. Sure, he was widowed now, but there wasn't a woman with him nor were there any more feminine clothes. There would be just panties. He packed his boxers, and was very grateful to Charlene for finally finishing the laundry.   As he drove to Huntsville, to the airport, the voice of the judge in the dream came back. "You must decide what you are. We cannot process you as you are now." He shivered. It was going to be hard. He was a woman in drag traveling among men. He was unsure about the repercussions. Some of the guys in sales were real assholes about sex, women, and anything different. He really didn't get along with them to begin with, and giving them further ammunition would not be a good thing. Then there was the gauntlet of two trips through airport security, rest rooms, and the ever-present other possible disasters lurking in everyday American life. His knuckles whitened on the steering wheel as he drove south. He dropped his car off in valet parking and took the shuttle bus to the airport. He felt people watching him. He handed his bag too the red cap with a twenty and went to the check in desk. As he finished checking in, his bladder started to make full feelings. It was crunch time! At home, he got used to sitting down to pee. Here he had to use the men's room. He was a man. He had female equipment, but his paperwork and clothing said man. He prayed for an empty men's room. It was not to be. He went to the end stall, dropped his pants and sat down. A river flowed forth. It sounded unmistakably female. He hoped no one would notice as he wiped himself and pulled up his pants. He was relieved that nobody was paying the least attention. Even though the echo of the sound he made was echoing through his mind. He successfully negotiated the first gate of the gauntlet.

This was the first time he had traveled since 9/11. Airport security was considerably different. Where there were a couple of bored Pinkertons before, there were uniformed officials and machines. He had to empty his pockets and take off his belt. He was nervous as he walked through the metal detector. It didn't beep. He picked up his stuff and walked to his gate. Gate two of the gauntlet successfully negotiated. It could have been much worse. He had heard tales of strip searches of ordinary businessmen. He was relieved that he wasn't chosen for that privilege. He took his seat in first class as the plane boarded. He had taken coach on that flight once. Since then, he took first class, as the little single aisle puddle jumper jet was cramped in coach.

Some engineer thought that it would be possible to put an extra row of seats in coach where there was only room for two rows. First class had two rows. The seats were the same, but there was no shared armrest and no close proximity passenger. It made the extra fifty dollars well worth it. It was the usual bumpy low altitude southern Appalachian flight. It took thirty-five minutes of flight time and half an hour in the holding pattern over Hartwell Airport. By the time he got off the plane and into the terminal he had to pee again. Huntsville Airport was basically a glorified bus terminal. Hartwell was a huge metropolitan international airport with its own mass transit system. The rest rooms were about a hundred yards apart, and as he remembered, always crowded. The first one he came to was out of order. He just barely made it to the second one. His stream started before he even got completely on the seat. Luckily, he missed his pants. The noise this time wasn't as disconcerting, because there was a steady babble of conversation and ambient elevator music. He checked again for watermarks as he pulled up his pants. He felt relieved that there were none. Gate three of the gauntlet successfully negotiated.

He retrieved his bag and set out for the rental desk. Even though he had reserved a car in advance, by telephone, it took two hours to process one out and get on the road to downtown. It was rush hour. It was another hour and a half when he pulled up to the door of the hotel. He had to pee again. He gambled on his ability to hold it until he got to his room. He wet his pants in the elevator. He was glad that he was alone. He started to cry. That hadn't happened to him since second grade. He was teased mercilessly about it for weeks. He let himself into his room and finished draining his bladder in the toilet. He pulled clean clothes out of his suitcase and took a shower. Gate four of the gauntlet: failed! As he was drying off from his shower, he caught a glimpse of his profile in the mirror. There was unmistakable evidence of breast growth. It startled him, as he wasn't taking hormones, and they were growing anyway. They weren't quite to the A cup size, but there were noticeable pert little teeny bopper breasts sprouting from his once masculine chest. Memories of the day the Sears guys came gave him pause. That was the first time he had conceived playing a female role. He was becoming female, whether he wanted it or not. It was inevitable. It was in the mirror. The male persona had become a lie.

22 Atlanta Dreams

The many years of hotel life caught up with Ben. He defeated the temptations of the mini bar., then he scanned the selections on the television. HBO was running Transamerica. He fell asleep shortly after the roadside urination scene. He was exhausted. As he slept, he found himself in a similar movie. Some of it was a re-run of the previous day. Some of it was straight out of the movie. Most of it was centered on finding proper places to urinate. Ben and Ted were traveling cross country. It was young Ted, about 16. Ben was in his present state though, and Ted was unaware of it. Current Ted was still unaware of it anyway, so it played into the dream. It followed script for a while until they came to a large inn, somewhere in the Midwest, probably Omaha, as the surrounding architecture suggested that city. The Inn didn't fit Omaha though. It was a massive brick pile, set above the street and disappearing into the trees above. A very old woman with a stern face greeted them at the desk. They registered and were directed to their room. Their room was on the fourth floor. It was a walk up. The wide center stairway was the route to their room. Their room was a farmhouse bedroom out of an old Western movie. It had a closet, but no bathroom. Ben needed to urinate. The building seemed to expand exponentially while Ben searched for a bathroom. As he searched, the urgency got stronger, and the interior landscape got stranger. The hotel became the Winchester house, crossed with an Ivy League College main building. The commonality was no bathrooms. Ted was with him, and he didn't want to reveal his changed anatomy to him, as he was afraid of damaging his relationship with him. He did not want to be seen urinating in his present state. Panic was welling up in him, as he searched. Then the scene abruptly shifted to the upcoming stockholder's meeting. He was standing behind a curtain while the Chairman

Covenant Roman Catholic Church

was introducing him to the meeting. Just as he was about to emerge from behind the curtain, he discovered that he was naked. Not only naked as in dreams before the cancer, but naked as he was at the present moment, breastlets and all. Walking out on stage, his bladder let loose of its contents.

He got up and went to the bathroom and emptied his bladder. He was thankful that he didn't wet the bed. As he walked back to the bed, the voice of the judge again told him that he must decide. Ben was tired. Sleep was chasing him. He crashed violently. The dream came back. People were laughing and pointing their fingers. The honoree had become the butt. They laughed at the little breasts. They laughed at the puddle on the dais. They laughed at his shame and humiliation. The taunts from second grade came back. He was naked as a woman and had no place to go. The dream didn't stop there. Marjorie walked in waving the prosthesis. "Hey Benny, you forgot your manhood!"

she yelled, as she walked through the crowded meeting room. He took it from her and tried to insert it. It still wouldn't go in. His vagina was too tight. The crowd started yelling "Benny is a virgin!" They kept it up as a group chant. The prosthesis became a large black strap on dildo as he held it in his hand. It squirmed like a snake as he held it. It hissed at him. He screamed and dropped it to the floor beside the puddle of urine. His toenails were painted a pale lavender. He looked at his hands. They were the hands of a second grader, but the nails were painted bright red. He screamed again but couldn't run. He was stuck to the floor. The crowd was starting to throw balled up pieces of paper at him. Then pennies. They chanted, "Dance girl dance!" It got louder, and more pennies rattled to the floor and bounced off his body. "Dance! Dance! They yelled. "Come on tiny tits, Dance!"

Ben woke up with a start. He was sweating heavily. The dream was still echoing in his ears. He started to cry. The mini bar called his name. He again refused it. He had had a bad experience with booze in Atlanta before, and this wasn't a time nor a place for another such experience

23 Stock Holders Meeting

At nine O'clock Monday Morning, the stock holder's meeting was called to order by the CEO. The top tier of executives and the honored guests were seated on a dais at the head of the grand ballroom in the hotel. Ben, being one of the honored guests was seated there. Normally, he would have been seated on the floor with the rest of the stockholders and other interested parties. He was retiring from the company, so this was also a retirement party for him. His Zero Gravity Servo was the main moneymaker for the company. It was involved in every aerospace contract, every military contract and most of the industrial contracts worldwide. Ben's urinary issues weighed heavily on his mind. It was customary for all the people seated on the dais to remain seated until officially sanctioned breaks. Ben's urinary tract was a patchwork of grafts, because everything between the sphincter on the bottom of his bladder to his pelvic floor had been removed with the cancer. The section of urethra in his penis was taken to fill the gap. To present as more or less normal, the doctors opted for a classic Gender reassignment surgery so that he had a socket to hang a prosthesis into, and still basically function as a male. It was his idea, but until the heat of the emergency cancer surgery, it wasn't taken seriously. Nobody in that hospital had done such a thing. Fortunately, a noted Somalian female urologist, specializing in female circumcision reconstruction was lecturing in the building. She was summoned and performed the reconstruction. The cancer had invaded even the pubic arch. A section of bone from a cadaver was grafted in place and the gap was spread just a little to flatten and widen the pelvis just in case the prosthesis didn't pan out, so he could seamlessly present as female if he wanted to later on. It left him with the urinary control of a mother of eight. He was seated on the dais with all eyes in the room looking at him, and he was wearing his last clean suit. Urinary emergencies had sent the other two to the dry cleaners. One by one, the CEO introduced the dignitaries on the dais. One by one they stood and acknowledged the introductions. The CEO fancied himself to be somewhat of an orator. In actuality, the staff of the company had other names and descriptions of him, most of which described moving air. People found any excuse possible to avoid meetings if he was expected to be there. At eleven AM he was still making introductions. Ben was to be the last. The CEO introduced Ben by describing the contribution he made to the company and gave an intro for the roll out of the new product line, which was Ben's baby all the way. He went on to describe Ben's tireless commitment to the company's image and bottom line all over the world with his one on one personal service to the customer all over the world. Ben could see the catering crew in the hallway pacing as the CEO droned on. Ben stood to acknowledge the introduction, sat back down for a respectful pause for the applause to die down and broke precedent. He left the dais. He bolted for the rest room. He barely made it. His boxers were damp enough to need to be changed. His pants survived. He balled up the boxers and pushed them into the paper towels in the trash can and headed for his room. On the way to his room, he dripped and there was a wet spot in the crotch of his pants. Fortunately, room service had gotten his other suits back from the drycleaners, so he changed his pants and went to the luncheon. The marketing people set up the seating arrangement for the luncheon. There were tables for ten in the grand dining room. Each seat was assigned. Each table had a bona fide company dignitary. Ben was seated with portfolio managers from a couple of insurance companies, a pension fund and a hedge funder from Greenwich Connecticut. The buzz word around the table was derivatives. This was an instrument for spreading risks on capital investments like mortgages and bonds to spread risk and raise money in a low interest financial market. These instruments used a complicated formula to cut each item into manageable pieces and knit them up into a commodified security. A complicated computer algorithm was used to set up the securities. Then the insurance for these securities was also commodified into other securities to further spread the risk. This was in turn re blended into the original securities in a fund, financed by the commodified securities. Nobody at the table understood the math involved but everyone thought it was the greatest thing since sliced bread, except Ben. There was too much room for fraud and over speculation for his taste. One of the older Insurance guys concurred. The CFO did the profit and loss statement during dessert. He explained the calculation of the dividend, and because of the start-up costs of the new product line, it wouldn't be as generous as it had the year before.

He urged the stockholders to hold on to their shares, as the new servo would revolutionize the market. He hyped and referred to Ben's upcoming lecture on the merits of the new technology and its effect on the industry. The luncheon broke up and the people moved back into the ballroom after a short break. Ben and Louie, the hedge funder left the table early and bolted simultaneously for the restroom to beat the lines. Ben barely made it. On the way to the ballroom, Louie said to Ben," We need to talk."

"Come to my room after the daily activities are over."

Ben sat in his chair and mulled over the events at lunch, and the sudden interest of the brash young hedge funder. He fought sleep as he thought about the global implications of these new instruments. The whole concept of the derivatives gave him the willies. There was no final accountability as to the safety of the initial investment, and the insurance instrument was rolled up into it as if it was expected that these shaky things would all eventually fail. He could not understand why this brash young man who worked with such stuff would be interested in talking to an old school buy and hold investor like himself. He was also preparing himself for the party that he was throwing in his room after the meeting let out. He figured Louie had heard about them and wanted to see what it was all about. At about three PM, He had to bolt for the restroom again. He never made it. He could feel it in his socks.

Church 24 Stockholders Meeting 2

Ben went back to his room and changed. He now had two suits for the dry cleaner. Again! He only brought three. He understood why Miranda packed so many clothes when she traveled. He used to tease her about it. Here he was, in the situation that made Miranda pack extra clothes- an incontinence accident. He showered, dressed and called room service to pick up his dry cleaning. He emptied his pockets, and put them on the desk. Room service knew Ben, so there was a bellhop at the door in about two minutes. He handed the bellhop a twenty and his suits, and locked up to go back to the meeting. Nobody said anything when he went back to the dais and sat down. He still had a major address to the stock holders the next day, asking for patience during the roll out. It wasn't just one product, but a whole line. The initial servo had been developed for NASA. The new one was smaller, and totally solid state. The relays, which made applications flexible, were gone. The logic board that held the relay was now a silicon chip.

The task at hand was to survive the rest of the day with no more incontinence accidents. He didn't have any more clean pants. He was supposed to entertain some larger institutional investors and a buyer from GSA in his room at the end of the day's festivities. He had already made the order through room service for Hors deuvres. He also had a bartender and a DJ coming up. There would be about twenty people in his room. He had done this before, and the parties were a legend around the company. It upset the sales people, as Ben wrote some sizeable sales through these parties. Now he was nervous about this last one. The room had only one bathroom, and though it was the biggest room in the hotel, it still had no real privacy. He knew most of the guests, so that he could almost relax. At six o'clock, the meeting adjourned for the day. Ben stopped in the men's room and relieved himself.

Passing a bit of gas covered up his visit to the stall. It also provided an alibi for his sudden departure and change of clothing. People are much more forgiving about shitting one's pants as they are about wetting them. Ben could never understand the logic of it, but it was a proven fact of group psychology. Several other people had developed loose bowels from the luncheon, so there were a couple of other men waiting for the stall when Ben left it. At the elevator, he met the securities directors from Aetna and Mutual of Omaha, as well as the man from GSA and Lou. It was Lou's first experience with one of Ben's parties. He seemed lost in the group of corporate and government big wigs. He seemed unnaturally shy. The two securities directors were joking about life in Hartford, or the lack of same. They were also making the same cracks about the entire state of Nebraska. They were in Atlanta, or, as the city was selling on TV, Hotlanta. They were going to make the most of it. The bartender and the

DJ were already set up in the room, as Ben and the first guests arrived. The Hotel management knew how Ben did his parties, and worked hard at helping out. The food was set out, there was music playing, and there were drinks waiting for the better-known guests. Ben had given up alcohol about ten years ago, and picked up his club soda with a twist of lemon and moved to the door to greet guests as they arrived. He had known most of them for years. It was no secret among the guests that his holdings in company stock were almost as big as some of the larger insurance companies. As a stock holder, he was a true heavy hitter. He was also the noted expert on tech stocks in the group, as he had pieces of at least thirty tech companies in his portfolio. He also had pieces of most of the insurance companies that were represented at the meeting. These parties were an old home week to the guests. They talked about family and activities outside the business world. Pictures of children and grandchildren were passed around, as well as pictures of spectacular vacations. The food trays emptied and were replaced. The tip jars filled, and the liquor bottles emptied as the party hummed along. An occasional line of cocaine was passed around, and a couple of strippers came and did their thing. The king-sized bed made an interesting stage for them as they gyrated to the music. One of them was doing flips in the air, missing the ceiling by inches. Bets were made on her ability to both miss the ceiling and nail the landing on the bed. At about two AM, the party wound down and people left. Finally, it was only Ben and Lou in the room. Housekeeping would have their work cut out for them in the morning, but Ben always made it worth their efforts. The room was a total mess. Ben and Lou found themselves sitting side by side on the edge of the bed.

"What's this about transition and stealth?"

" I noticed an absence in your pants on the dais, no lump where there should be one, so I figured that you were also transgendered too."

"Well... not in the way that you think. I had cancer. I lost my reproductive system and the doctors gave me a vagina to use to attach a prosthesis. Unfortunately, I didn't know to dilate, and I can't put it in because my vagina shrank. I can barely put my thumb in."

"Oh, I thought you were like me. You are going the normal direction. Good luck anyway, it's hard."

"My problem has been bathrooms."

"For me, that has been the tip of the iceberg. Try finding someone to remove two healthy double D breasts. I still haven't found a surgeon to remove a healthy uterus and two healthy ovaries. The hormones make me crazy and sometime sick. I haven't found a plastic surgeon to make me some convincing genitals, so I use gym socks. The counseling alone was thousands of dollars, and cash doesn't work too well in the medical community. Hell, any back-alley butcher can whack off a penis and a pair of balls. All my stuff is inside, and then there is the matter of the hole between my legs. It has to be closed right, or infection will start, which could be fatal, or at least destroy the work on the surface. If I didn't own a hedge fund, I couldn't do this."

"That's ironic. We are meeting in the middle. Up until today, I thought that I could stay male, even with a vagina. There you are, another man with a vagina, at the same place and the same time. Actually, we are both women in drag. Today, I discovered that, even without hormones, I'm growing breasts. I'm not sure what to do about it. They are still small, and easily concealed."

"You are going to have to choose sooner or later. I chose seven years ago. As a man, for some reason, people trust me with their money. As a woman, they never did. My fund has twenty thousand investors. Most of them came on after I lowered my voice and grew whiskers. Except for being short and small, nobody has questioned me."

"This is the first time I have been out of the house since a woman pulled off my prosthesis in Nashville. She totally freaked out, but now, she's my friend. Up until now, I didn't know much about it. I am learning stealth the hard way. Up until last year, I had occasional fantasies, but never took it seriously. Now, I'm living with this fear that I can't quite explain. Up until last year, I was married with three kids and a couple of grandkids. I was totally male, and never thought about it ever being different. I worked all the time to hide from Vietnam. I ran a swift boat and got shot up several times. If I don't totally exhaust myself, I wake up screaming. I made it a point to not be home very much, because it upset my wife. I ended up neglecting her and my health, now I am becoming a woman, and can't do a thing about it."

"Look, if it's any consolation, neither one of us chose to be this way. I'm hardwired to be male, yet I was born female. I figured it out when I was about five. I noticed I didn't have the proper equipment to be a boy, I freaked out. I was sure I was a boy, until I saw one naked. My parents and relatives tried to tell me but in my heart I was a boy. I still am."

"Where are you staying?"

'The Ramada over by the airport."

"Wow, that's a long haul for a short night. This is a big room with a big bed. Why not stay here?"

"I don't know, all my luggage is in my room. "

"What do you need out of it?"

"My hormones, and underwear."

"I can get underwear from room service for you.

"What kind do you wear?   "

"Tighty whities."

"That's easy."

"What about my hormones?"

"We'll go chase them in the morning. The meeting starts at nine."

"You don't mind, do you?"

"We share a secret."

"Yeah, I guess we do."

"We need to crash! It's going to be a long and busy day tomorrow!"

"The bed's a mess."

"Yeah, there were nude dancers on it"

"I guess there were!"

"Look on the bright side, they took their shoes off."

Lou went in and took a shower. Ben called room service for some medium Fruit of the loom knitted men's underpants in white. They were delivered before Lou got out of the shower. Ben knocked on the bathroom door and put them on the vanity. Then he straightened the bed. He found a hundred and fifty dollars in the bedding.

24 Charlene and the Prosthesis

Charlene decided that while Ben was away at the stock holder's meeting, she would dust his bedroom, vacuum and wash the bed linens. Ben lived in his bedroom, the living room sofa, and the kitchen. He rarely visited any other parts of the house, and since he was feeling better stopped changing the bed. He would put his dirty clothes in the hamper in the bathroom, he didn't really dirty many as he really didn't do much. He ate, a little. He slept, fitfully, in bursts, wherever he landed, and he read the financials, from the newspaper, Forbes, Money, and a couple of obscure trade journals. He would make occasional long telephone calls, and go to his doctors. The bedroom was a mess. The ceiling was full of cobwebs. Every horizontal surface had a coating of dust. There was a drift of Kleenex on the floor beside the night table. Some of them were bloody, as if he was having nosebleeds. She had been itching to clean the room for weeks, as she sensed that if his surroundings were neater he would feel better and would want to go someplace besides his doctors or Miranda's grave. She hoped that the stockholders meeting would kindle a much-needed spark in his being, as he seemed terribly depressed. It seemed like it was more than mourning. There was something else at work too. As she walked into the room, she noticed the prosthesis on the nightstand. She was surprised to see it there. He was in Atlanta. It should have been in his pants, not on the nightstand. The back of it was smeared heavily with Vaseline, streaked with blood. She picked it up. She had a certain trepidation about handling it as it still gave her the willies from her time living with Marjorie, and their surgery on Sid. It looked so much like the object they had set in Lucite. The blood mixed with the Vaseline bothered her. On closer examination, she noticed Vaseline mixed with blood on some of the Kleenexes.

"Omigod, she gasped, He couldn't put it in and went to Atlanta without it!" She took it in to the bathroom and cleaned the mess off the back. The blood had dried into the Vaseline, and hardened into a cement like substance. She could imagine the pain that would result from bleeding that much in the place the prosthesis belonged. "Why would this thing make him bleed there", she asked herself. She cleaned it to the bare plastic. And examined it. There were no sharp edges, no projections except the catheter. The catheter was clean except for the sterile catheter lubricant that was used on it. She pumped it erect. It worked perfectly. It stayed erect for about ten minutes until it slowly deflated to its flaccid state. The ball end compressed easily. She made a circle with her thumb and forefinger and forced the ball end through it. It moved through easily, even without lubricant. She decided to try it and see what caused the blood. She slipped off her slacks and panties and stood at the sink. She lubricated the catheter with the catheter lube, and inserted it into her urethra. It was tricky as she had never done anything like that before and had never been catheterized before. It stung a little as it went in, but moved in smoothly. She pushed the ball against her cervix and it slipped in effortlessly. The last inch went in with a slap as the flap at the base slapped against her labia. It felt strangely good, though just a little cold inside her. The catheter in her urethra gave her the urge to urinate. She walked over to the toilet and flipped up the lid and urinated through the prosthesis. It felt natural. She returned to her housekeeping duties, wearing the prosthesis. She realized that with the prosthesis, she couldn't wear any of her slacks nor could she wear her panties without stretching them out. She dug in a dresser drawer and pulled out a pair of Ben's boxer shorts. With a couple of safety pins, she shortened the waist band so they would stay up. It wouldn't do to have visitors walk in with her walking around half naked with male genetalia. Her slacks still wouldn't go over the prosthesis, as they were too tight in the crotch for more than a vagina and a pair of panties. She put on a skirt. She giggled as she slipped into it. She felt vaguely guilty. The cut of the skirt was such that there was a lump in the center of the front. She dug through her clothing some more and found a pleated skirt with a wider taper to it. It clashed with her top, but concealed the prosthesis between her legs. Moving around with a foreign object in her vagina stimulated her, and she squeezed down involuntarily. The outside of the prosthesis jumped a little and pushed against the fabric. The little push against the fabric fed back into her vagina and it squeezed involuntarily again. She felt a tingle she had never felt before, and the prosthesis pushed back again harder and the front of her skirt pushed up a little. The weight of the fabric on the end of the prosthesis pushed harder into her vagina and she squeezed again. The tingling got stronger and she felt a moistness inside. She squeezed down harder. The prosthesis was now fully erect. Her hips were moving involuntarily, and she was starting to feel really hot inside. The tingling inside her vagina was turning into a feeling she had never experienced before. Proper New England Catholic girls don't masturbate, and she had followed the rules. Her hips were totally out of control and were thrusting back and forth with wild abandon. She felt a contraction from way deep inside her. Then another and another as her uterus shared the orgasm. She felt weak in the knees. Her legs were just barely able to support her as she stood in the doorway, doing an involuntary dance. She felt a wetness running down the insides of both legs. Then it was over. She walked rubber legged back into ben's room and flopped across the bed. The prosthesis was still erect as she fell forward across the bed. The pressure on the rigid member pushing on the inside of her vagina triggered another orgasm as strong as the first. The flap pushed on her clitoris and she jerked and twisted on the bed. A big wet spot appeared on the front of her skirt, as her uterus contracted again and again. She had never before felt such pleasure.

In the back of her mind, she wondered about the source of the blood. Why did something that generated so much pleasure in her, and probably Marjorie before her, cause bleeding in Ben, the proper owner? The second question was why didn't Ben take it to Atlanta?

25 High Rollers Only

The second party at Ben's place was a calmer affair than the first one. There was no DJ, and no dancers. There was a simple self -serve bar, and a modest buffet. It was a business meeting for institutional investors, and a strategy session for maximizing dividends. Lou was there as a guest because he was staying with Ben. He was the only hedge funder. His eyes were opened to the opportunities of true investment over time. There was much talk about the magic of compounding and the leverage it generates over time. Lou was fascinated. He had never really thought about keeping stocks for long periods. Long term investment was a mysterious realm that was inhabited by old fogeys that didn't believe in computer generated trades. About midnight the party finished up, and everyone left. Lou was amazed at how Ben worked the room, moving from small group to small group, shaking hands and slapping backs. His knowledge of business cycles was the best Lou had ever seen. Very little of it was in textbooks. The change in clothing for the last part of the meeting shocked the crowd. It was unexpected. It also got him more attention. They hung on every word at the meeting. The move from Pascal to UNIX platform was explained in dollars and cents saved in code writing for interfaces. The servos could be triggered from anywhere through the magic of the internet. Because everything was solid state, electrical demands were simplified. The lack of a jacket and tie made him more convincing as a hands-on engineer. It was a sales pitch made in heaven. For two hours, the only sound in the meeting room was Ben's voice. When he finished, there was long loud applause. It was a fitting last act to a long career. Now, Ben and Lou were alone in the room. Room service had taken away the remnants of the self -serve bar. The buffet was left to the chambermaids in the morning. There were a few refugee shrimp, a couple of finger sandwiches, some cold cuts and some rolls. Ben and Lou nibbled on them as they talked.

"That was the best business class I ever attended!

"They don't teach that in business school anymore. Everything is short term now."

"After hearing you talk on the subject, I am suspicious of my degree in business, and I have an MBA."

"I have an engineering degree. I never went to business school. "

"Where did you learn so much about business?"

"Doing it."

"But you were going into the stratosphere of high finance."

"I had to justify my job and support a family."

"But you were doing corporate finance. That

isn't taught in business school."

"I had to justify new products from the field to the bean counters in corporate by showing how they could be financed, and made myself a retirement in the process."

"They treat you with a reverence I have never seen from a bunch of stock holders."

"To be in this room you have to hold at least twenty thousand shares of our stock." That's a current value on the market of ten million dollars. I am sitting on thirty thousand shares myself. Figure it out in common stock at three hundred and seventy-five dollars a share. I get between ten and fifteen dollars a share every quarter. I used it for years to buy more stock. I have a nice portfolio as when this stuff is real high, I will sell some and buy stock in other companies. I have no idea about what my net worth is, as I have never had to pay capital gains yet. I live on my salary which is nice, and part of my dividends."

"You only pay taxes on your salary?"

"Well, a little from my dividends too."

"Why, if you re-invest them?"

"It keeps the IRS off my back."

"Do you have anything else going?"

"Just that. I can't spend all the money I make. Why make more?"

"How about your family?"

"I set up a trust for education that if it's prudently used should go for ten generations."

"No, I meant income."

"They're better off without it. They don't know how much money I have. I plan to keep it that way. They fight enough already."

"What are you going to do with it?"

"Frankly, I have no idea."

"Let me get this straight, you have this huge sum of money stashed away, and you have no idea as to what to do with it. You gotta be kidding me!"

"I never thought about it. I was too busy earning it and investing it to think about it...until now. When I came up here during the meeting to change clothes, it hit me. I am an old lady with more money than anyone should have. Yes, a lady! I am very new at being a lady, as I surrendered to it just a few hours ago. There is nothing male left in me, except some chromosomes in my cells. On top of that, I'm menopausal. I have hot flashes. I'm moody. I cry easily over nothing. I have grandchildren. Now I'm a grandmother instead of a grandfather, and they don't know it. It's so fucked up!"

"Hey I'm sorry to have stirred all this up....."

"Hey, it's OK, I'm glad I'm not alone here right now. You have no idea how much time I've spent alone in hotel rooms. Now I have nobody to go home to. No, I take that back there's the girl that came to take care of me when I was really sick.

Actually, she takes care of the house, and leaves me my space. It's nice having her around, but she's the same age as my kids, maybe a tad younger. I never asked."

"Anyway I know you're exhausted. I'm beat too. I'm going to take my pills, and go to bed. It will be the first time as a man, I have gone to bed with a woman, even though she is old enough to be my mother. We really need to do something about clothing. We can't have an old lady walking around in menswear."

26 Shopping

Morning again found them in a knot in the middle of the bed. They weren't as embarrassed as the morning before because it felt good. Both had expressed the gnawing loneliness that possessed their lives. Both realized that it wasn't sex that drew them together, but a sense of common humanity and shared experience. They lay together and relished the feeling. Ben got up first. He had to empty his bladder. He was on the edge of leaking. He just barely made it to the toilet. As he sat there, the weight of his realization hit him. He started to cry. The emotion tore through him as he sat on the toilet. He was a female, ignorant in the ways of women. He had no clue at all on how to continue his life, and this was permanent. He had no control over it. It was grief tinged with regret. None of the roles he owned and was accustomed to would work anymore. He sat and wept bitterly. Even his name no longer fit. There was no Ben here anymore, and the person sitting on the toilet didn't even have a name. She was a cypher

Covenant Roman Catholic Church

to him and the world; a nameless sixty some year-old woman sitting on a toilet in an expensive hotel room with a man she had only known briefly. To compound things, this man was a woman in the process of becoming a man, and still had mostly woman parts. It was confusing, ironic and just plain sad. He wished it was different. He was totally lost. There was no familiar real estate here. The hotel might as well have been in Dubai, as downtown Atlanta. The visual landscape was the same down to the wrapped glass on the sink. Even his memories no longer fit his/ her body. They were a man's memories. He now fully understood Helga's mention of the price he paid, but where was the true love he had paid for. He had paid a terrible price. He had paid with his identity. The prosthesis on his nightstand at home was now a lie. He saw that now. Eventually he would have to abandon it anyway. It never worked right for him in the first place. He couldn't take the hormones that made Lou male, because they would awaken the dormant cancer cells

191

hiding everywhere in his body. He would, like it or not have to embrace his new gender, and function in the world from now on as a woman, without the benefit of being a girl first, and without a name as a point of reference.

Lou needed to use the toilet, and after a lot of time passed, he thumped on the door.

"Hey in there, are you still alive?"

"It depends on who."

"What do you mean?"

"Ben disappeared last night. For all intents and purposes he's dead."

Covenant Roman Catholic Church

"Who are you then?"

"I really don't know. I don't have a name anymore."

"Omigod! I understand. I spent a lifetime preparing to change roles. My female role was temporary and I daydreamed this role from almost the beginning. This was dumped on you over less than two years, and you resolutely clung to the old roles and name. We have a real problem!"

"I'm sorry I dragged you into this, I really am!"

"No, no, it's OK. Who else out there would understand, much less be able to help. After my mastectomy, I went into a severe depression. I had cut off my link to my feminity. My therapist and my surgeon had warned me about it, but it still hit me hard, and I already had a name for the new male being I was creating, but I still wanted to die."

"I'm in so much trouble…."

Covenant Roman Catholic Church

"Look, I want to help you. Very few people truly would understand what is happening in you. I only understand because I am an ex-woman, some man's ex -wife. I failed as both a wife and a woman, and now I am trying to be a man. You were a successful man in all the ways it counts to society. You had wealth power and family. Yesterday you simply stopped being a man. You still have everything else, but you are a woman now. I think I can teach you to be successful as a woman, if you will let me. There isn't anyone in Greenwich waiting for me. All I need to do my business is a phone line. I was a woman for a long time. I can teach you how to function. First we need to call room service and get you some warmups, so we can go shopping and get you outfitted as a woman. We will have to work from the skin out. I am going to shave, put on some makeup, and don some warmups too, so I can go into the dressing rooms with you. We're both going to be ladies for this exercise."

Covenant Roman Catholic Church

"I don't know about that... the credit cards?"

"Are any of yours joint with your late wife?"

"The Macy's card."

"We'll go to Macy's"

Ben called room service and ordered two warmup suits from the gift shop, one in women's large, and one in women's medium. Then they started to pack. Room service brought up two warmup suits. They were matching blue and white Danskins nylon with zippered jackets. They put on the warmups and finished packing. Ben telephoned the front desk and checked out over the phone. He added a hundred dollars to the tab, each for tips, for room service, the valet who was going to have the car waiting at the door, and for housekeeping for the extra work caused by the two parties in the room. They took their suitcases and went to the lobby. Ben handed the valet a twenty and they got in the car and headed out. The first stop was at the drug store for a compact and a lipstick. Lou became Louise again in about five minutes. It took a little longer to feminize Ben's face, but a little bit of powder and some lipstick worked wonders. A pair of sunglasses finished the quickie makeover. Then it was off to Macy's. They started in intimates. They bought two three packs of padded bras, one in a 40 and one in a 36 Ben tried the 40, and Lou changed it for a 42. After a little twisting and adjusting, it fit. Lou started calling Ben Mom. Ben smiled at the idea and went along with it. They went to sportswear and bought slacks and blouses. Ben selected a lime green mock turtleneck in a smooth cotton blend. He became Mom when he slipped it on. He matched it with a pair of tailored tan slacks, zippered up one side with a button on the waistband. He no longer resembled a man in any way. He became Mom. They bought a short grey carefree wig. Louise fitted it to Mom's head and smoothed it out. Mom was now Mom for everybody. They each bought a little black dress and a couple pair of shoes each. Mom decided on a pair of black patent leather pumps with a three-inch heel. They actually had a size twelve wide in stock. Louise was nervous as Mom tried them on. They looked really good and Louise was happy that Mom didn't try to walk in them. They fit perfectly so they were wrapped up with everything else. Mom kept the green top and tan slacks on as well as the wig. They stopped at the makeup counter and set up makeup kits for the new handbags. While they were looking at handbags, they bought appropriate wallets. Nobody batted an eyebrow as Mom signed Miranda Slackmeyer to the credit card receipt.

"I don't want to fly back to Huntsville like this."

"What do you mean?"

"I can't do it."

"You nailed the presentation yesterday and last night, you owned the place, and you can't get on an airplane and fly home?"

"If I manage to make it through security with the boarding pass and my ID, which doesn't in anyway match me, I still have to behave in a way I never learned how to, as I have only been a woman for a few hours. People will stare."

"I forgot about security at Hartwell. I think you're right, and there is no way we can get another ticket without matching ID. The ticket you have is worthless too for the same reason."

"I guess we drive back. We have another three hours on the rental. Let's buy a car for the trip. That way I can get used to my situation before we have to deal with any more authority figures or need ID."

"You want to buy a car?"

"Sure it makes sense. We deal with a car salesman, I call the bank, and we drive out of

Covenant Roman Catholic Church

the dealer with a new car."

"How about registration?"

"Temporary plate. We're going to Tennessee. I'll register it there."

27 The Long Trip Home

The salesman at the Ford dealer was a total asshole. He talked down to the ladies, and tried to sell them stuff they didn't want or need. After twenty minutes of telling the jerk to just sell them the car, they walked out of the showroom. The Chevrolet dealer was nervous about a wire transfer to pay for the car as he had never done one. After arguing about finance and GMAC, they walked again. The Dodge dealer didn't have a car ready to go, but they would give them a great deal tomorrow. They bought a Nissan Maxima. The salesman knocked three thousand dollars off for cash and no trade-in. The deal was done and a temporary tag was affixed to the car in fifteen minutes and the salesman didn't even check for a valid driver's license. He was happy to make a sale. They dropped off the rental and headed east toward Birmingham. In Talladega, they stopped for a late lunch at a diner. It wasn't hunger that made them stop, it was the need to drain. They had peed at the rental agency at the airport, and with traffic, it was a good two and a half hours on the road. They emptied their bladders, adjusted clothing and makeup and ordered lunch. The cashier, noticing the new high end clothing and the brand-new car did what any public-spirited citizen would do if they saw something out of the ordinary. She called the cops. Two Alabama State police officers showed up and asked for ID. Both licenses said male. It had taken Lou's Lawyer and a friendly legislature a year to get male on Lou's license. Lou was wearing a grey Verchasse pant suit, a string of pearls and a pair of black patent leather flats. The picture on the license had a moustache and a pinstripe business suit. Mom, AKA Ben's picture was three years old. He had short gray hair and a five o'clock shadow, as he noticed his license was about to expire and rushed out to renew it. He was wearing a blue tennis shirt in the picture. Mom

AKA Ben was still wearing the green mock turtle neck and the tan slacks and had on a pair of topsiders. Everything fit perfectly. Two more officers showed up. They weren't as polite as the first two. They had all kinds of questions they wanted to ask. The two traveling ladies were detained and their car was impounded. Sol Weinberg's phone rang.

"Hey Sol, Ben here. I am in Talladega. These officers think that I am up to no good and they arrested me because they wouldn't believe my ID. They think I stole a bunch of lady's clothing and a new car, or bought it with dirty money. They have me and an associate locked up on Money laundering charges. We were just driving back from the stock holders meeting. We stopped for lunch."

"Put the officer in charge on the phone for me."

Covenant Roman Catholic Church

"OK but I am pretty sure that you might need to come down here. They aren't pleased with us. They are accusing us of using stolen ID's. They also confiscated our cash."

"Put the officer on the phone, and I will straighten this all out."

"OK, but I' really don't think you can do it over the phone."

"Hello, I'm Lieutenant Henshaw. These two ladies claim that they are men and that they earned all that money legally. They are wearing all new clothes and are driving a brand-new Nissan with temporary plates. Even their handbags are new. We want to know where they got the ID's and the money, credit cards and merchandise. We also want to know what happened to the owners of the ID's"

"The guy I talked to is Ben Slackmeyer. He has been my client for over twenty-five years. I talk to him on the phone all the time. He lives up

Covenant Roman Catholic Church

here in Sterling Forks. I assure you he can afford all that stuff and he earned that money".

"No, these are ladies, the older one smells like my mother. There is no way in Hell that her name could possibly be Ben Slackmeyer."

"I'm warning you right now, if you guys don't release those two right now, give them everything back, and apologize, you personally will be homeless, naked and walking for the rest of your life, and the press will make a laughingstock out of your division of the Alabama State police. I know that is Ben. I don't know what is going on with him, He recently lost his wife and came close to dying of cancer. He has severe PTSD from Viet Nam. He's a decorated naval veteran. He is also an aerospace engineer. You have an hour, or I call the press."

"But these are ladies!"

Covenant Roman Catholic Church

"Ben has a top-secret security clearance with the Federal Government, and is a veteran. Run his prints."

"That will take three days!"

"If you book them, or interrogate them any further, they have grounds for a large false arrest suit, as well as a suit for harassment. They have the money and connections to win against anyone you can hire to represent you. You have an hour, or I will start the paperwork, and call the national media. Northern Alabama looks bad enough already for harassing motorists. It's a running gag in the movies. Do you want to be a laughing stock?"

"I know the difference between men and women. These two are women!"

"Let them go!"

About that time, the Captain came into the booking room. He saw the two women on the bench, and the lieutenant arguing on the phone with a lawyer.

"What's going on here, Henshaw?"

'We picked up these two ladies in a diner, trying to pass themselves off as men, and carrying too much money. We think they are drug dealers or worse. I am talking to the older one's attorney, a Sol Weinberg, right now. He insists that their ID is legit."

"They look like ladies to me too. Did they do anything wrong at the diner to attract attention?"

"I don't know. It was a suspicious behavior call from the cashier, before they ordered."

"What kind of suspicious behavior?"

"All new clothing and a brand-new car with temporary plates from a dealer in Atlanta."

"Let me get this right. You guys arrested two ladies for stopping for lunch in a new car because they were wearing new clothing."

"Their ID's didn't match them."

"Did you have probable cause for checking ID's?"

"They looked suspicious."

"Look, Henshaw, if your mother and sister went on a shopping trip to Atlanta, and bought a new car there, would you want to see them stopped and booked as Jane Does?"

"No sir."

"I suggest that you get their car from impound, and bring it here, escort them back to the diner, and buy them lunch. I don't give a rat's ass what their ID says. Buying lunch in a diner while wearing new clothes is not suspicious behavior. You didn't have grounds to even check ID."

"Look at them. They are traveling with two men's ID's"

"They could be crossdressers. Have you ever heard of drag queens?"

"But they're actually ladies...."

"You don't have legal grounds to even check. You are already skating close to a false arrest charge. Do you want to spend a year on unpaid leave while it grinds through the courts? I can't spare five guys from this barracks for a year. Follow my orders, or I will cite you for insubordination."

"What about the damage the search team did to their car searching it for drugs?"

"You what?"

"We searched their car for drugs"

"What did you find?"

"Nothing but some testosterone pills in a prescription bottle."

"Did the name on the bottle match either ID?"

"Yes sir."

"Then there was no contraband was there?"

"No sir."

"You guys took a brand-new car apart and found a legal bottle of prescription pills."

"I'm afraid so, sir."

"Do those two people look like Thelma and Louise to you?"

"No sir."

"Do they match any profile for drug dealers to you?"

"They had a large sum of money on them."

"Did you have a warrant to search them?"

"No sir."

'Did they flash the money conspicuously in the diner?"

"No sir."

"How did you figure that they were carrying a large sum of money then?"

"We searched them."

"What would you do if that happened to your mother?"

"I would be angry. I would probably help her sue the people responsible, sir"

"Take the car to the Nissan dealer and get it fixed, then get them a loaner to finish their trip. And buy them lunch, and anything else they want. I don't want to go down with you guys for the charges that they can bring on you. I also don't want five of my guys on unpaid leave while the case ties up the court. I have seen Sol Weinberg in action. You don't want to be on the receiving end of it. I certainly don't. Now get moving!"

Mom, AKA Ben, AKA Jane Doe, and Louise AKA Lou AKA Jane Doe 2 checked into the Holiday Inn, in Talladega. Mom's panty liner and slacks were soaked through. They were both exhausted from the ordeal with the police. The lieutenant picked up the tab for lunch and the motel with his own credit card. He was very apologetic. One of the arresting officers carried their bags into the room. He wouldn't make eye contact. He kept looking for things on the floor. He left without a word. Mom showered first. As she stood under the hot water she started to cry. The afternoon had been too much for her. She still didn't have a name to match her persona. Ben Slackmeyer obviously didn't work anymore. The attention by the police proved that. She wept bitterly for the mess her life had become, and the loneliness she saw in the future. She had become Thelma. She was on the run. She even had a Louise with her. She went from crying to laughing hysterically. The scene in the booking room after the fact was just too much. The Keystone Kops couldn't have been more inept. It was definitely an adventure.

"Hey Lou, I found a name. Call me Thelma! We'll be Thelma and Louise!"

"That's a good one. I guess you earned the name. I don't think Mom is an operative name anyway. Thelma, it is!"

'Why don't we wait for the car to be ready, so we don't have to hassle with the loaner when we get to Sterling Forks? Talladega is a really beautiful place. Let's play tourist."

The morning found them in the familiar knot in the middle of the bed. This time Thelma was spooned around Louise's back. It was a blissful feeling laying there. Neither one wanted to move at all. Only the urgency from their bladders caused them to rise from the bed. They dressed and put on their makeup and went to the lobby for breakfast. They were wearing the warmups from the hotel in Atlanta and Topsiders. They looked all the world like mother and daughter. The lobby was busy with tourists. Thelma and Louise ate their continental breakfast and went out to the car.

"Have you ever heard of Talladega Lake?"

"No. What's that?"

"It's a huge lake in a very scenic spot. It's a

natural wonder in these parts. I used to come here to fish occasionally. My son, Ted loves it here."

"I've never paid attention to things like that. I grew up in Greenwich, and went to New York or to the casinos for recreation. I've never been fishing."

"Never?"

"I've lived most of my life indoors. I didn't fit in, so I didn't go out much. I play the stock market. It's both an occupation and recreation. I do that, and go to casinos. I like poker."

'Yeah, I can see that. You're a born gambler then."

"Yeah. I gamble. It's my main vice. I don't smoke, I don't drink, and I'm still a virgin, except for that one asshole"

"You never dated afterward?"

"I prefer women anyway. I always did. The problem here was, I really didn't like most of the lesbians I met. I wanted a normal heterosexual woman. I didn't want to play the gay game. I also didn't like the glass ceiling in business. You have no idea how hard it is to convince people that you are the wrong gender so you can do something about it. I started hormone therapy with black market steroids. I almost died from them. I found a therapist, and started transitioning. I also started the hedge fund to support the transition. It's all expensive, and none of it is covered by insurance. My hormone treatment is about a hundred dollars a day. Then there's voice training and counseling. I go to group therapy once a month in the East Village. My life revolves around my transition."

"You can go back to your normal self now if you want."

"Yeah, I'd like that. I forgot how much I hate wearing makeup. Besides, I have nothing to hold my bra up anymore. It rides up and feels strange. I didn't particularly like wearing it in the first place. Since the mastectomy, it's just wrong. I can still teach you while being a man."

"I don't expect to go shopping for clothing in the near future. Dig out your regular clothes."

Two hours later, Louise was back to being Lou. It was an amazing transition. Here was Lou, the Connecticut tourist, dressed in an IZOD tennis shirt, White Dockers, and a pair of Gucci loafers. Gone was Louise, the Gold Coast princess. It was good. Thelma gave him a hug. Lou helped Thelma dress and do her makeup. Thelma still had little experience with those things. She didn't even know how to sit in a chair right. They chose the dress for the day's activities. It took half an hour to struggle into pantyhose. Thelma practiced walking around the motel in her high heels. Lou laughed hysterically. Eventually, Thelma figured it out and developed self-confidence enough to leave the motel and go into town. They stopped at a coffee shop and had lunch. Thelma had trouble remembering to cross her legs when she sat down. A couple of gentle kicks under the table reminded her. As they walked down the street, they walked past a big mirror. Thelma was amazed at her reflection. She was actually a fairly good looking woman. She was tall, but except for having a flat ass, even with the heels, she didn't look bad. They picked up some souvenir T shirts, and a bumper sticker. They paged through post cards, and window shopped. After about an hour, Thelma had enough of the high heels. They went back to the motel and changed into something more comfortable and appropriate for travel. At about three O'clock, they called the Nissan dealer about the status of the car. A couple pieces of plastic trim were broken during the drug search, and weren't in stock. The car would be tied up until the parts came in the next morning, and were installed.

"Call back at about noon tomorrow", said the service writer.

"I guess we play tourist some more"

"How about the National Forest. You are from the densely packed East Coast. You have never seen the stars. I know a nice restaurant in the middle of it where we could have a nice meal and then go out and really see the stars."

"How far is it?"

"About thirty miles or so."

"Might as well, except for the racetrack, we've mined this town out."

"The attraction here is the big lake and the racetrack. This place was a wide spot in the road until TVA built the dam."

"Well, let's go!"

The trip up Mount Cheaha was uneventful except the scenery and the wildlife. They talked about the Market, and the revolution sparked by computer trading. They discussed strategy in selecting stocks and how to bargain hunt in NASDAC. After paying a modest admission, they entered the park. The forest service took good care of this portion of the park, because it was busy most of the time. It was well groomed clear to the lodge. The lodge was impressive. It was at the very pinnacle of the mountain. The view in all directions was amazing. From there they could see three states. They walked around the lodge admiring the view for a while and watched the hawks circling above them in the air currents off the mountain. Finally, they entered the building. The inside, like the outside was native stone. It was accented with natural wood and modest furniture. They took a table and sat down. The waitress brought a menu.

"Y'all wantsumta drink?"

"Yeah, we'll have a couple of Ice waters."

"Y'wantsmlimmininit?"

"How's that?"

"D'y'all wunts sum limmin in it?"

"Oh, Lemon! Yes please!"

The waitress went to get the drinks.

"I couldn't understand a word she was saying."

"You get used to it. The farther out you go around here, the heavier the accent."

"Yeah, I probably sound funny to her too."

"I've eaten here before. The ribs are amazing, and they have pulled pork. They also have the best steamboat roast beef I have ever eaten. It's slow cooked over an open fire, just like the pulled pork."

"Sounds good, but I was thinking of something lighter. How's their fried chicken?"

"It's old fashioned pan fried. It's moist and juicy. But it tends to be a bit greasy. It's not your usual fast food fried chicken. It comes with the best coleslaw in the South."

"What's their catfish like?"

"It's fresh caught wild, breaded in cornmeal and deep fried at a very high temperature. It is addictive. It comes with Texas fries. I don't think you can finish the plate. It's a huge serving."

They settled on the steamboat roast beef for Thelma, and Lou ordered the catfish. The roast came with a huge baked potato with sour cream sprinkled with wild ramp, chives and parsley. The catfish was served on an oval platter on top of a mountain of Texas fries. It was so tender and delicate it was hard to pick up with a fork. Lou had eaten very little freshwater fish, as he grew up in Connecticut, where most fish for sale was from the sea. The catfish melted in his mouth and tasted better than any fish he had ever eaten. Then there were the fries. An Idaho potato displays mystical qualities at 500 degrees. It is also the only way to properly cook Texas fries. At a lower temperature, they don't cook evenly. They end up raw in the middle. Because catfish also requires very hot oil, the Texas fries had the mystical quality found only above 500 degrees. It was dark outside when they decided to order a container for the leftovers.

They walked outside to the car and dropped off the containers. Then they walked down the gravel path to the observation deck, a hundred yards away from the building. The moon wasn't up yet, but it didn't matter. The stars provided more than enough light to navigate the path. The observation deck was slightly higher than the surrounding terrain, and far enough away from the trees to provide a horizon. It was a clear night, so the stars put on a better show than usual.

"Now that is the proper night sky. This is one of the few places in the country that you can see it in all of its glory. That river of stars there is the Milky Way. That is the galaxy we are living in. that W shaped formation over there is Cassiopeia. That big square is Pegasus."

"I never looked at the night sky before. I couldn't see it if I wanted to. I've never been away from the street lights. This is amazing!"

"I thought you would like it. It's almost this nice in Sterling Forks. It's on the edge of the Andrew Jackson National Forest, so there isn't much development east of town. My house is about as far east as development goes. It sits on four acres. I have a single light on the house beside the front door, and one above the center garage door. I can walk outside and see the stars. I never did it as much as I wanted to. I was never home. I was always working somewhere else."

A tear ran down Thelma's cheek when she said it. The stars blurred in her vision. Lou, seeing the change in posture, pulled her close and held her around the waist. He was moved to tears from the sheer beauty of the night sky. They both stood looking at the sky in silence. A meteorite zipped across the sky and disappeared. The eastern horizon brightened as the moon rose. It wasn't a full moon, but it didn't matter. It was still big and bright as it cleared the horizon. Eventually they got cold, and walked in silence, arm in arm back to the car. Morning found them spooned in the center of the bed again. Thelma rose quietly, used the bathroom and returned to bed. Lou stirred a little when Thelma climbed back in and spooned around him. She needed the warmth and contact. She knew Lou did too. Finally, daylight and Lou's bladder woke them from their comfort. They woke, dressed and went to the lobby for the continental breakfast. They sat and watched the other tourists. There were different tourists from the day before. They were race fans. The uniform of the day was baseball caps and T shirts. Lou's beard was coming back from two days of too close shaving. There were a couple of ingrown whiskers. Thelma watched him as he ate his breakfast. He wasn't the Gold coast princess any more. The change over two days was amazing. His posture and mannerisms were different in subtle ways. His manner of speech was different too. A subtle kick under the table reminded her to be more ladylike in her posture. She crossed her legs.

At

about ten, they called the Nissan dealer. The car was ready to go, so they swapped out the loaner and brought it back to the motel and loaded their luggage. At noon, they were back on Interstate 20 heading west for Birmingham. They ate lunch at a little dive beside a gas station in Birmingham. The Pulled pork sandwiches were really good. They were messy to eat, but worth it. The little dive had a big neon sign saying BBQ. It was the smell of it that drew them in. They picked up Interstate 65, and headed north. The northern outskirts of Birmingham were ugly. It was nice to get past them into the north Alabama countryside. This was horse and cattle country. Green pastures with grazing animals slid past the windows. Lou watched it go by in awe. He had never seen open country before, much less grazing animals. An occasional large pond passed by. They went past patches of woodland more now as they neared Huntsville. There were also more ponds.

"What are those ponds about?"

"Those are catfish farms."

"They raise catfish commercially?"

"Yeah, it's a growing business here. It's more dependable than wild caught. The fish are more uniform and there is no mercury in the meat."

"Mercury?"

"Catfish are bottom feeders. They vacuum

stuff out of the slime on the bottom of any body of water they inhabit. Mercury comes out of the air from burning coal, and leaches out of the soil upstream. It concentrates in the life on the bottom of any body of water that is surface fed. The mercury is concentrated in the flesh of the creatures that eat stuff off the bottom. There is also industrial and household waste that leaches into our waterways. Stuff like fluorescent lights and TV picture tubes. Mirrors and electrical switches also contribute to the problem."

"I never thought about stuff like that."

"Nobody does."

"Hey, we are in Tennessee!"

"How much farther?"

"Not far at all. Just three exits now."

Charlene was weeding a flowerbed in the front yard when she saw a strange car with two people in it pull into the drive way. It was a new Nissan with a Georgia temporary tag on it. It pulled up in front of the center garage door and stopped. A tall woman and a shorter man got out. They opened the trunk and pulled out suitcases. She recognized one of them. It was Bens. She had helped him pack it over a week ago.

27 the Common Book

Francis held the common Book in his hand. Tears came to his eyes as he considered it. A piece of the song came to his mind about the troops gathering them up and burning them because they were in "devil script".

"This book is the creation of John Calvin, founder of the Presperterian Church. Our people happily accepted the beliefs, and Jesus Christ, because the missionaries preached a thing called predestination. It meshed seamlessly with our beliefs. We know the Great Spirit has a plan for us to tend Her creation. It was translated into Cherokee so everyone could benefit from it without having to learn English. This was rough country. Travel in some parts here is still difficult. Sequoyah and the Elders translated the Common Book and the Bible into Cherokee using the new Syllabary. By the great uprooting of the 1830's, there were hundreds of churches dotting the countryside. For some reason, the troops didn't burn very many of them. A lot of them still stand today. Many of them are still used as churches. They were built by and for the Cherokee, but there are very few Cherokee to worship in them, and the worship isn't in the Cherokee tongue anymore."

"You have seen these before then?"

"I have one just like it in my rig. I use it to worship the Great Spirit, and to Love My Savior."

"You have another one?"

"It isn't as nice as yours, but I do. It was Sequoyah's copy. It has been re bound several times. There are a few more at Trail's End in Oklahoma. They don't use them, because our language was banned by Federal law. Very few people speak it anymore. I do, because it's my duty to carry the Song of my people."

"Song?"

Covenant Roman Catholic Church

"As you would say, oral tradition of our Nation. It's our history from the beginning. Until I find a willing student to pass it to, I have to keep singing it in its entirety. The Common Book is part of it. It's the only part written down."

"Why didn't you pass it on to your children?"

"I didn't have any. There were no Cherokee women here. I have to tend the holy places, and can't leave the area for very long. The English women didn't want a Cherokee man. I never married."

"Why not?"

"I am a Shaman for the Family. A wife has to follow our traditions and ways. The English women's families were afraid, so they wouldn't let their daughters be with me. They were afraid."

"Afraid of what?"

"It was a federal offense to speak our language and honor our traditions off the reservation. The reservation is in Oklahoma. All our holy places are here."

"Are there any other Cherokee around here?"

"Sure, several hundred. There used to be millions of us. Our Nation. Stretched from Canada to central Georgia, and from the Atlantic Coast to the Mississippi. There were twenty-six tribes." When Andrew Jackson's troops rounded us up and marched us to Oklahoma, we were indistinguishable from the English, except for the use of our language and traditions. We owned property, had slaves, grew cotton, spent money, just like the English. Jesus Christ was our Savior too. We were the largest Prespertary in the entire Church. We still honored the old ways too, as they meshed perfectly with Calvinism except a few stupid things about sex and gambling. Our elders couldn't find anything against them in the Bible, so we ignored them. They weren't in the Common

Book either. Our Language didn't have a male word for The Great Spirit. Our language doesn't have a word for ownership or possession. Until the English came, we had no need for them."

"Do you have much contact with them?"

"Sure, they are all relatives."

"All of them?"

"My great great grand dad, Bearclaw, outlived six wives. He sired over forty children with them. Any Foster in the region is a relative of mine."

"Are you passing all that along to someone?"

"I have a grandnephew. He has been initiated into the ritual."

"Ritual?"

"He was anointed by the Elders."

"I thought that the tribe was effectively gone from here."

"Yes, the Tribal government is in Trail's End Oklahoma. The Holy Places are here. The Elders inhabit the Holy Places. The eternal life in the Gospels is real. The missionaries didn't tell us anything we didn't know before, except Jesus and the power of love and forgiveness. We already knew about eternal life."

"Who are the elders?"

"The shamans from generations past. They are in the Holy Places. So are the people of the long past. We honor them by tending the Holy Places for our children's children."

"How do you tend the holy places?"

"We do it by keeping things from changing except by natural causes."

28 Fred's Dilemma

Fred was not prepared to start another major project. Compost had bits and pieces of inspirations that at one point or another looked good, but crashed into walls at closer inspection. Nothing was ready for prime time. He had a couple of seriously X-rated pornographic short stories, a how to cope book called *How to Be Happy, a Manual,* and several other odds and ends of fractured prose. *How to Be Happy,* was a takeoff on the movie *Beetlejuice.* It was written like stereo instructions in a dense format. It crashed at two chapters. It was a skewed look at sociology. It was funny and insightful. It had one serious flaw. Fred wasn't happy when he wrote it, hence the wall. The pornographic short stories were about a couple in their seventies dealing with a stale relationship and no sex. They sat there because he didn't want to sully his reputation by going to the magazines that would publish them. Now he needed income. His publisher had effectively fired him, and probably blackballed him from publishing as well. Maybe the fact that he had published a best seller would open the door. He enjoyed writing pornography. He had a rich fantasy life, and could come up with some really good images as well as put sensual feelings into words. He felt that that genre was beneath his upbringing and education, so he never seriously pursued it. Now, the wolf was at the door. There would be no more royalty checks. The best seller was out of print, and his new book was sitting in a warehouse in Chicago, probably forever. Because Sterling Forks was basically still a Bible College town, there were no pornographic bookstores in town and the various venues that sold magazines didn't even stock Playboy. He had no Idea as to where to send his stories. He hopped the first bus to Nashville. He hadn't been out of Sterling Forks since he stopped touring the circuit with the best seller. Nashville was a whole new world, as a lot had changed since he'd been there. He spent a whole day writing stuff down from the fronts of various magazines. A lot of them had no real printed stuff, just pictures and descriptions of the women in them. He cringed at some of the titles of the magazines. He had been in Puritanville for too long. Nobody had anything about geriatric sex written in them. He bought copies of *Bitch, Grunt, Love Pit, and Tease Me.* They had stories in them. *Bitch* was locally published. *Grunt* and *Love Pit* were out of New York, and *Tease Me* was out of L.A. He saw on those magazine shelves a huge market for his hidden talent. There were also a vast number of books. He had leafed through a few. If he applied himself, here was steady work. An experienced and talented author could stay busy and make a living in that market. He was talented and experienced, and an author. He pulled up the two stories out of Compost, and hit print. He got half of a page, then empty sheets. The printer had run out of toner, He

wrote and saved the necessary cover letters and
went to the college bookstore where he still had a
charge account. They were out of his cartridge.
They would have more in a week. The end of a
semester wasn't a good time to look for laser
cartridges in a student book store. He went back
home and further studied his magazines from a
purely literary standpoint. His sophomore fiction
class did better work. Even the sex was rote and
formulaic. He came to a decision. He was going to
turn the literary pornography world upside down.
He was going to submit actual stories with plot and
story arc to the readers of smut. Then he was going
to break into the big three, Playboy, Hustler and
Cosmopolitan. He left it all on the coffee table.
There was no need to hide them. He knew that
Marjorie would get a kick out of it. He then dug into
Compost and dug out a piece of work called *The
Tattoo*. It was a story about a couple in their
seventies whose sex lives had stopped years ago and

the husband was impotent even with Viagra. He was tired of one way sex and took a unique solution to the problem with a tattoo around his genitals and a threat to have them removed if he didn't get some form of mutual pleasure. It got really pornographic in its description of how the wife tried to preserve the status Quo and her husband's genetalia against his will. As he read it, he smiled. It was a good opening gambit for the world of literary pornography. Length might be a problem as he didn't think the readers of porn had the attention span for a novella length work in a pornography magazine that pandered mostly pictures and whose ad revenue was from mostly telephone sex providers and sex toy manufacturers and retailers. Satisfied, he curled up on the couch and took a nap.

Covenant Roman Catholic Church

30 Miranda

The twenty-fifth anniversary party was a fiasco from the beginning. Neither daughter showed up. Neither daughter answered the invitation at all. There were no cards from either daughter acknowledging the event. There were sixty-five people invited. Miranda and a local caterer had prepared for seventy-five people. Over a hundred showed up. All of them friends and acquaintances of Miranda. The stress of the big event started affecting her about a week out. Miranda dealt with the stress by fortifying her iron resolve as usual with alcohol. Her medicine of choice, dark rum. Her husband as usual was out of town doing God knows what for the corporation. She really didn't give a rat's ass what he did at work. She wanted him with her. For twenty-five years, she had an absentee husband. He traveled through the big house leaving very few traces. There was a razor on the vanity, several suits and shirts and stuff in the closet, underwear in the dresser, but very little evidence that she even had a husband. Her drinking was disguised as an innocent glass of Coke on the counter, always just under half full. There was a two-liter bottle of it in the refrigerator. It was 1/3 rum. The giant Cuba Libre had been a fixture in the refrigerator since Ted had started school. She forbade her children from drinking any carbonated beverages. The big Coke in the refrigerator was for guests and the occasional tradesman that came by to fix stuff. There were few guests, and fewer tradesmen, but the children believed the lie anyway because they were afraid to question anything she said as her wrath was terrible. The children toed the line or else! Her little secret vice was safe. She was a functional drunk. She did what she was supposed to and much more to compensate for her empty life. She had given up television as it mocked her very existence with its constant barrage of marital bliss. All it did while she watched it was expose her broken American dream of a husband and children in a big happy house. The big house was far from happy. It was a mausoleum on a cul de sac in the middle of nowhere. It was a maintenance headache. Her only creative outlet there was the yard. She hated the house, but didn't want to mention it to her husband as she was afraid he would resent her disrespect of his hard work and sacrifice that bought it, and not come back at all. She was lonely. Most of the time, she was also bored. She buried herself in church work, gardening, and Cuba Libres. Her children kept a respectful distance, as any appearance of rebellion was dealt with harshly with any object at hand. She never struck exposed skin after the school nurse called about some bruises on the oldest daughter's legs. To the outside world, her children were perfect. They were the envy of every parent in the church. She worked very hard to maintain the image of control and a functional alcohol level outside of the house. Occasionally she would slip and melt down, but it was usually when she was alone. She knew her life was irretrievably broken, but she had no one to confide in to help her fix it. Outwardly she had a perfect life to match her perfect figure, maintained by many forgotten meals and heavy yard work. Reverend Henry saw the edges of the loneliness and did what he could to alleviate the pain. He had seen it before in his congregation. Intelligent women forced into the role of housewife instead of using their hard-won college degrees to better the lot of the world, acting out their empty lives in negative ways. He could count at least sixty active alcoholics, twenty-five drug addicts, and several women that acted out by gossiping to hide sexual misconduct. He was trained in seminary to see it and deal with it as a pastor. In the meantime, he could see is own marriage falling apart at the seams from the same neglect that brought the women of his congregation to him for help. Miranda was special to him. She was the smartest one of the group. She was a Radcliffe graduate with a degree in Botany with a minor in Economics. She had graduated with honors, then ran away with a sailor and got married, to escape a hellish environment at home. She was always perfectly dressed with perfect hair and makeup. Her children were models of perfect behavior. He had only seen her husband a couple of times, and wasn't sure if he could even pick him out in a police lineup. At first he thought the husband was a fabrication to cover up illegitimate children. Lots of women wore wedding rings without the requisite husbands to go with them. At first he suspected that with Miranda. Then he saw the house and knew she couldn't have a house like that without either a husband or a very wealthy sugar daddy. She did talk about her husband, and the stories seemed convincing. There were the phone calls when she was doing things in the church office. There were the postcards from exotic places that she brought in to show off. There was the exotic wardrobe that went with the postcards. Outwardly it was the perfect suburban life. She had the big house, the perfect children, and a seemingly endless supply of money. Yet he sensed just a little despair and desperation. There was an occasional unsteadiness in her walk and a clinginess in manner. He couldn't minister to his congregation without her. She filled in the gaps in administrative duties around the church. Sure, she occasionally drove up on the curb when parking and occasionally backed into things when leaving the parking lot. She was a smallish woman driving a Cadillac. He expected things like that.

The first five years of the marriage were idyllic. He was pursuing an electrical engineering degree at MIT. Between her job as a sales person at an insurance agency and the GI bill, they lived fairly well. He obviously loved her. They had children within a few years. By the time he graduated, they had three. He spoiled them rotten. When she came home from work, all tired out, they were disobedient and disrespectful, as small children are when supervised in a hit or miss manner by a busy father. She saw her own childhood repeated in them if she didn't take action. The children feared her and soon were obedient to her wants and needs. As a successful mother, she needed perfect children. When her husband graduated, and went to work, she left her job and became a full-time housewife. Three preschoolers in a row house in Boston was her lot in life until...NASA needed a relay that would work in a pure oxygen environment to switch large currents in space for the arm on the Space Shuttle. It had to be light and hot swappable in space with minimal tooling. Her husband designed such a thing on her kitchen table. He got a bonus and a transfer to Huntsville Alabama. The job wasn't in Huntsville, though, Just the office he worked from. Otherwise, He traveled to sell and adapt the relay to other applications, all expenses paid, worldwide. Anywhere there were flammable gasses there was an application for the relay. It found its way into oil refineries and gas plants as well as flour mills and coal mines. He went to the site, checked out the specifications and designed relays for it. He trained people to install and change them and drew a commission. She learned very quickly that money was no substitute for physical presence and love. The only plus was her husband was too tired at the end of a tour to wake up screaming from his experiences in Southeast Asia. He slept soundly and was affectionate in the morning. When they first got married and started to live together, he would go for days and days without a good night's sleep from the night terrors. She didn't get much sleep either. She started anesthetizing herself with rum. It helped her sleep through his night terrors. It also helped her deal with the trauma of being raised by a domineering and combative alcoholic mother and an absent father. Her grandmother saw what was going on in the house and rescued her, but the damage was done. At Radcliffe, she discovered rum. Rum quelled the voices in her head that told her she was no good. Rum soothed the angst from not quite measuring up to the standards of irrational people. Rum was the warmth that her mother never gave her. Rum was her salvation and her downfall. Her grandmother paid her way through college. She strove hard to make it work. She graduated with honors. It almost killed her.   To handle the workload and the lab work, she added Dexedrine diet pills to her self-medication regimen. She stopped menstruating. With the Dexedrine, the voices came back, so she drank more rum to make them go away. She buried herself in her work. She spent the summer in the psych ward. She weighed eighty-two pounds when she was admitted. The next fall, the Dexedrine was gone from the regimen and replaced with cocaine. Her grades stayed good. She checked into Detox the next summer. She was a level five addict. She had burned through over twenty thousand dollars. She was on the dean's list again, but had no friends and hadn't ever been on a date. The senior year she did rum, coffee, cigarettes and amyl nitrate. She met a sailor, fresh from the Mekong Delta. She graduated, but never returned home. Even with the sailor, who obviously adored her, her life felt empty. She medicated the emptiness with rum. Corinne was two and Deidre was four months old when she had her first blackout. She tried to drown Deidre. Corinne ran for help to a neighbor. Deidre was hospitalized and was on oxygen for a month. Her husband never knew about it as he was working and going to school full time. MIT is a tough school. Corinne never trusted her mother after that. Neither did Deidre.

Miranda demanded that her children be perfect in every way. Her idea of perfection and perfection in children are two vastly different things. Corinne and Deidre reacted to the gulf in different ways. Corinne rebelled. Corinne got punished for it. Deidre acquiesced. The near-death experience taught her that she had to toe the line no matter what. Eventually, the two girls presented to the world as perfect children. They held deep resentment and bitterness from then on. Ted was raised from babyhood in Huntsville. It was a different world than the row house in Boston. He had two experienced mentors to teach him how to keep on the straight and narrow. His main desire was to please those around him. It also helped that most of the time, he was the only male in the house. Even as a small child, it made a difference. If any child disturbed the equilibrium, they all suffered. Corinne and Deidre worked hard to keep Ted out of trouble. Deidre took the lumps for all of them. Corinne was rebellious and oppositional, especially if she thought that their mother was wrong. They all worked hard at keeping up appearances. They looked like the perfect happy family. For all intents and purposes, Miranda was a single mother. She saw her husband one weekend out of six. He was usually suffering from jet lag, but he brought back exotic gifts from all over the world. He slept most of the time, but didn't have night terrors very often any more. It was wonderful having him sleeping beside her, quietly snoring sometimes. She soaked up his smell and his warmth like a drought survivor. She didn't need rum. She had him. He spoiled the kids. They were loud and rambunctious and he loved every minute of it. Miranda knew that they would be wild for a couple of days after he left and dreaded it. When they were wild they weren't being perfect children.

Covenant Roman Catholic Church

Then he would be gone again. As the kids reached school age, Miranda had doubts about the Huntsville schools. She had a picture in the back of her mind about the South. Schools were a great part of it. Perfect children went to perfect schools. She needed more culture than she thought Huntsville could provide. She stumbled upon a magazine article about Sterling Forks Tennessee, which was billed as the college town of the future. Diversity and culture were the buzz words. She had never heard of Sterling College, but that didn't matter. It was a college town within an easy commute to Huntsville, and it was in a dry county. The temptation for liquor wouldn't be there. She was becoming frightened by her dependence on rum to function and worried about her health. The college billed itself as "A New England College in the South". The Sterlings had come from Boston, and the plantation buildings reflected their tastes. So, did the town, which was centered on a white

Congregational church, just like a New England postcard. They bought the biggest lot on the new subdivision east of town. They built a grand house. They had New England money at south central Tennessee prices. Money was no object. They had lots of it. It had six regular bedrooms with attached baths. A master bedroom with a room sized closet and a matching guest room with a similar closet. There was a huge ultra-modern kitchen with all the modern conveniences. A good crew could run a four-star hotel restaurant from it. It had a large formal parlor, a matching dining room, a family room, and a library. It had an attached three car garage leading into a walk-in basement that housed a laundry, a general-purpose room and a large mud room. It also had a wine cellar. It had a sunroom on the south side attached to the kitchen. It had a state of the art climate control system that controlled both temperature and humidity to a steady state, year around. It was on a cul de sac. Beyond the

Commented [JH1]:

yard was forest. It was a suitable home for a Boston Brahmin. Unfortunately, Miranda wasn't one. Her grandmother was. The breeding and culture were beaten out of her by an alcoholic mother, an unknown father and a lifetime of drinking. It was a maintenance headache for her from day one. It took the services of two cleaning ladies twice a week to keep it clean. The house had to be clean for the cleaning ladies so the kids couldn't really be kids in their own house. It was isolated. It was ten miles out from town. It was the first house in the development, and the College people lied a lot in the brochures. The college ran the schools, so they seemed OK. If the truth be told, it was still a Baptist Bible College in the middle of nowhere that expanded its curriculum to take advantage of GI bill money. They needed diversity to make it look good. Hence the ad and the brochures. The college was there because the Reverend Sterling got a bargain on the plantation buildings during the Great Depression. His dream was to produce preachers for his radical sect of the Baptist Church that used live venomous snakes in its religious services, and spread his True Faith Baptist Church all over the world. It wasn't a sustainable business model. Hence the expansion after forty years to a liberal arts college. The trap caught the Slackmeyer family. The kids found that they could escape their mother for days at a time by simply being quiet and moving about the house. It was a big place with many hiding places for children. The girls slept together at first, because of habit. They had always slept together. Soon, space and petty differences sent them to different rooms. Ted slept as far away from the girls as he could, because he didn't like to listen to them fight. They always fought over everything. Corinne was noisy, opinionated, stubborn and messy. Deidre was sullen, withdrawn, moody and obsessive about neatness. They only had each other for company.

Ted lived in the library during almost every waking moment. He didn't interact with his sisters at all. They both beat on him both physically and verbally. His main motivation was to please people so as to not get beaten. He only felt safe when his dad was home.

When they moved into the big house, the yard and grounds were a huge mud flat, strewn with construction debris. Nobody had even thought about landscaping. It was what Miranda needed to straighten out her life. She discovered gardening. She put her Botany degree to work to make the grounds match the house. It was also the best thing that ever happened to her children. They got to play outside in the dirt. The mud room had a shower and could be hosed clean. Their mother was occupied with the lawn and grounds and didn't pay as much attention to perfection in her children. The Botany degree and her fascination with plants gave her a constructive outlet that she never had before. She stopped drinking except for a nightcap after a heavy day of outside work. She dragged all the construction debris into a hole she dug in the middle of the yard and set it on fire. After it burned, she filled in the hole. She raked the area smooth and brought in topsoil. She raked that out and planted grass seed, selecting grasses that matched the light conditions and the soil conditions as there were several limestone outcroppings on the grounds. She mixed white clover into the seed mix to provide nitrates to the grass. Then she started with shrubs, trees and beds. She had an outlet for the boredom and loneliness of being a housewife. She also had a magnificent lawn and grounds. She joined the Congregational Church and became active in that too. It gave her a social outlet. It was still ten miles to anything though. Her husband bought her a Cadillac. The children grew. There were two television stations reachable by the antenna. There also was no cable service. The children learned to amuse themselves without TV. A satellite dish was discussed, but dismissed as just too much trouble for questionable entertainment value. Corinne dropped out of high school in eleventh grade and ran away with a boy on a motorcycle. She never wrote and never visited. Only Ted knew of her whereabouts, and he was sworn to secrecy. Deidre got pregnant in tenth grade and ran off to Beale Street in Memphis with a saxophone player twice her age. She sent baby pictures, but little else. Ted graduated from High school and went to Vanderbilt to study Engineering. He came home to visit occasionally, but never moved back home. Miranda took a job as a financial planner at the local insurance agency and gardened. She had her perfect house and perfect garden. Her only visitors were her husband and people from the church. The years went by.

The anniversary party was set up in the big

parlor and adjoining dining room. A buffet of hors deuvres was set up in front of the fireplace in the dining room and small tables were scattered around set up for four or five people each. Each table had fresh flowers on it. Two music students from the college, one on the piano and one on violin provided the music. No expense was spared on the décor. Miranda was celebrating her perfect family. She assumed that because of the significance of the occasion, Corinne and Deidre would come, even though she hadn't heard from Corinne for years and communication with Deidre was directed by Deidre's husband, because he felt that family mattered. Deidre never talked about her childhood with him. Deidre never visited home. Deidre never voluntarily called. Deidre didn't RSVP when she got the invitation. Deidre didn't tell her husband about it either. Except for the usual pre-party disasters involving food and punctuality, things went smoothly. Miranda was still nervous. They never had any sort of big shindig together. She had no idea as to how her husband would behave at this one. They eloped when they got married. They never really socialized together. She had no real idea as how he behaved in large groups. She started a second two liters. She had shared some of the first with the caterer, but had drunk a reasonable amount herself. By four o'clock, when guests started arriving early, she was in her zone. Her husband, who was due in at ten, still hadn't arrived. He had called from Winnipeg the day before and assured her he would be there. She gathered, arranged and placed flowers, checked place settings and bustled around, but inside the insecure little girl that couldn't do anything right was scared shitless. She fortified her courage with more Cuba Libre and worried. She entertained the early arrivals, made small talk and made them comfortable. She made a dash for the bathroom off the kitchen and vomited. It was streaked with blood. She had forgotten to eat again. She ate some saltines and some cheese and brushed her teeth and rinsed. Her mouth still tasted like regurgitated rum. Her stomach hurt. She ate some more saltines and some pretzels and went back out to the guests. Her legs felt rubbery as she walked to the living room. More guests came. She bustled around, made people comfortable and made introductions here and there. It was six o'clock. Her husband was still a no show. She was starting to feel angry and abandoned. She was celebrating twenty-five years of being married to a ghost. He was never there. She needed him now, not just to trot out to show to the guests, but to hold her and tell her it's all O K. She needed a hug and a pat on the ass. She needed kind words from the father of her children, her lover and her spouse. At seven thirty, he arrived carrying his two suiter and his carry on. He had a two-day growth of beard and smelled like a locker room. His clothes were rumpled from time spent sitting on airplane seats. He looked like he hadn't slept in a week. He was definitely not ready for a big party in their honor. He was home! She almost knocked him off his feet when she wrapped her arms around him. Her dark depression immediately changed to joy. He hugged her back and kissed her.

"Happy anniversary Miranda"

"Where the hell were you?"

"They cancelled the flight from Chicago to Nashville. I ended up flying into Anniston and renting a car. The rental agency didn't have one ready to go so I had to wait for a car from Huntsville. It was a mess. Then I hit construction on 65."

"You said you would be here this morning"

"The flight from Winnipeg was delayed."

"We have over a hundred people here to celebrate our anniversary, and you are very late and you are never here when I need you."

"I'm sorry dear. I got here when I could."

"Don't you I'm sorry dear me! I've been planning this shindig for months and you don't care enough to show up on time. We've been married for twenty-five fucking years and most of my friends have never seen you. Her voice got louder.

"You left me here in this God forsaken mausoleum in the middle of nowhere with three bratty ungrateful kids, two of which didn't care enough to answer my invitation to come today. You missed Ted. He was here, but left. I'm here with all these fucking people, trying to explain the lack of family at a twenty fifth anniversary party. How do you think it fucking looks? I've been a single mother for twenty years! I raised those fucking bastards all by myself! Two of them didn't stick around to finish high school! All the work sweat and worry, for what? I'll tell you what! A half hour visit from a preoccupied college student, who came, ate, and screwed, and a husband that didn't care enough to show up on time: a husband that is a ghost at best! Everyone here has at one time or another thought I was a loose woman and had three illegitimate children because they never saw any evidence besides the ring that I was even married. You come here now and again to fuck me, and then you go traipsing off to God only knows where to do God only knows what. To you, I'm just another whore you fuck to keep your prostate clear. You drop me into this mausoleum to give the appearance that you care, but when I need you, I can't even call you on the phone. You call me, when you goddamn feel like it, and talk for a few minutes, and then hang up. I needed you, and you weren't there. You are never there!

She started to cry.

"Calm down, honey, I'm here now. I'm sorry! I've done the best I could!

"You miserable bastard! You think showering me with presents and stuffing me into a big house is loving me! It's not! It's just more dusting and sweeping! I have to hire people to stay on top of it. I'm stuck in the middle of nowhere in a town that serves a snake handler seminary! I have to go to Nashville to get my hair done right. My nail polish is mail order because nobody down here stocks my brand! I can't even watch a Red Sox game! There's no culture here! I hate it! I hate you! I would rather die than live here with you for another minute! I don't want to be here!

"You can't mean that. Can you?"

"I mean it! I mean every word! Can't do this anymore. It feels like I'm living a lie. I don't have a husband I don't have a family. Nobody loves me! I want to die!

"Hey, Kid, I've loved you ever since I first laid eyes on you. You are the beacon that lights my way through the world. It's you I think about in the lonely hotel rooms every day I'm away. I'm so sorry that you feel bad. Soon I'm going to retire, and I'll take you to all the places I went so I can share them with you. I need you as much as you need me, but I have to work. I'm committed! It hurts me to be gone so much!"

"You're just saying that because you don't want to look for someone else to fuck when you are between calls. You probably have whores or even wives all over the world. I know how that works. Who are you fucking when you are not here? What does she look like?"

With that last question, she ran upstairs and slammed the bedroom door. The guests scattered like midnight New York City cockroaches when the light is turned on. Suddenly the house was empty except for the Slackmeyers, the catering crew, and the two college students. The scene still echoed as Ben, AKA Mom, AKA Thelma carried the bags into the big house. Now she was gone, and rum was involved: shredded with a sailor in a freak train wreck right before Christmas. His/ her heart was heavy from the memory. He had spent the whole time he was home that time sleeping on the couch. He tried over and over to forgive her for the outburst, but she was cold and angry toward him. It was almost a year before she would be cordial toward him. They never made love again. The relationship was broken. Thelma sat on the couch and cried for the loss. Charlene could only watch. There was nothing she could do.

31Corinne's   Home   Coming

It was an easy decision for her. It was the third time he dumped his Harley. He was in a persistent vegetative state in a convalescent home. He had no medical insurance. He drank, partied and fooled around on her. They had been married for sixteen years, and it never got better. He resented the kids and worked when the spirit moved him. He said he loved her, but really didn't show it often. The last spill ate their meager savings. It was a year ago. He still refused to wear a helmet. Now he was a vegetable taking up a bed in a convalescent home with no hope of ever waking up. She walked out of the room for the last time. She had visited him every day, but she could see it was hopeless. Hell, he was hopeless from the beginning. She had put the wheels in motion for a quiet divorce. It would end the almost twenty-year financial drain he had put upon her. Because of him, she had nothing but two adolescent children. There was no furniture except a couple of Wal Mart futons and some plastic stacking chairs. The table was a half sheet of plywood on a couple of sawhorses. Everything came from either Wal Mart or Goodwill. Working three jobs brought in food, but not much else. His Harley and his habits took the rest. She lost count on the number of evictions. Her kids deserved better. She packed three suitcases and bought bus tickets to Sterling forks. She wasn't sure she would be welcome there, but it was worth a try. The bitch was dead. She couldn't bully her anymore. Dad was retired and last time she had seen him, pretty sick. She felt guilty leaving him in the hospital, but couldn't take any more time off work and really didn't trust her husband with the kids. Her father had been good to her. She felt bad about not saying good bye to him when she left home. Now she was admitting defeat and crawling back home. She was nervous. She had nothing but good memories of her dad, what few memories she had of him. When he was home, he played with her and read her stories. He lovingly tucked her into bed at night, and loved her just the way she was. He wasn't home much, but when he was life was great! He made her feel special. Many years had passed. Now she had kids of her own. Would they accept a grandfather that they had never met? Would he love her kids? Would he even let them stay? She left without a word. Would he hold it against her? Her stomach knotted thinking about it. Her son sat with his head against the bus window watching the Tennessee hills go by. Her daughter slept. Both of them were eager for the trip. There was nothing for them in Knoxville. Between them they had attended every elementary school in the county. All they had was each other. Corinne noticed that early and did what she could to help them ease the loneliness of being the new kids in school. She spent what little free time she had encouraging them and making them feel loved. They were going to a totally new world. She never told them much about her childhood. She described the house, but never much else except some of the good times walking in the woods with Dad and her siblings.

They changed busses in Nashville. The sign on the front said Birmingham. It went south on 65, stopping in every town between. They couldn't sit together on that one as they were late to the bus station and the bus was almost full. She worried that separated like that, one of them would get left behind on the bus at Sterling Forks. At the bus station, she saved out enough for the local bus to the suburbs and bought three hot dogs. They ate on the bus. The hot dog went down hard. Her knotted stomach really didn't want food, but she forced the issue as it was the entire nourishment for the day. It went down and stayed.

She wished she had money for drinks. The water fountain in the bus station was slow and filthy. As people got off the bus, the small family moved closer together. Thirst was the topic of conversation. The Sterling Forks bus station was the drug store too. The local bus service had a stop there. To get to the suburbs on the east side of town they would have to transfer at the college. The trip from Nashville to the end of Apostle Drive took almost five hours. It was another hour of lugging suitcases to get to the big house on the cul de sac. They stood on the front stoop as Corinne rang the doorbell.

A familiar looking older woman answered the door.

"Corinne!"

"Dad?"

"Yes!"

"What happened?"

"Cancer"

"But you're...."

"I gave up the "man" act after he stockholder's meeting. The cancer surgery was too radical to continue as a male seamlessly in society. It was all about restrooms and stereotypes. I'm so glad you're home! Come in and I'll find you something to eat. We have some serious catching up to do."

"You are still Dad, Aren't you?"

"That hasn't changed. I'm still Dad, and I will continue to love you as a daughter."

"Are you sure? I'm homeless with two children and totally broke. I abandoned my husband just like I abandoned you. I'm so ashamed. I ran away because I couldn't live with Mother anymore. I had two kids with a loser. I was ashamed to come back. When Mother died, I came back to see what I could do, but I got into a fight with Dee and someone called the cops. I have outstanding warrants for stuff I did for my loser of a husband. I couldn't stay. I'm no damn good."

"You have to be doing something right. You brought me grandchildren! You have no idea how happy that makes me. I haven't even seen pictures. I know how things get away and out of control. I was an absentee parent, as bad as any gangster in the ghetto. I wasn't there for you for any of your milestone events. I'm here now for you!"

"Oh Dad, if you only knew what it was like when you were on the road. She wouldn't let us talk about it. We had to be perfect children, or else. It's not your fault. You did the best you could. We had clothing and we were never hungry. In her strange and distorted way, she loved us. She wanted us to be the best we could. She was a damaged person and passed it on. I fight the impulse every day to achieve "perfection" in my kids. Then, when she died, I was so ashamed for my failure as a person. I figured that if I worked hard enough at it I could fix my husband. Then I could come back proud."

She started to cry. The little group in the doorway

clustered closer together.

"I have been praying for the day that my children would come back to me. This big house is a millstone around my neck because it's empty. It needs family. Since I left home to join the navy, I have experienced long periods of loneliness. Fear of loss made it worse. In the Navy, I made friends, only to see them killed in combat. I was in charge, so responsibility weighed heavily on me. Because I failed to keep the men entrusted to me safe, I felt like a failure. I pushed myself to success, forgetting to take time to just enjoy life. You, Deidre, and Ted are the bright spots in my life. So was your mother. I wanted you to have everything I didn't have. I squandered my time amassing great wealth. I showered my family with it. I drove all of you away doing it. I was so afraid of failure, I failed as a person. Let's get you settled in. You live here now! The house needs people in it. Your bedroom is just the way you left it. Neither your mother nor I could bear to move anything. Deidre's room is the same way. So is Ted's. Your kids can choose from any other unoccupied rooms there. I have a couple of guests, but they are set up in the guest room and my room."

On their way across the living room, they met Charlene. Corinne jumped. The resemblance to her mother was unsettling. There was a time when Miranda experimented with hair colors, and red was one of her choices. Corinne stopped and her pulse went up from fright. Then she realized it was a different person, but her heart was still in her mouth and her palms were sweating.

"Corinne, this is Charlene. She has been here since shortly after I came back from the hospital. She has been taking care of me and the house. I could not have survived here without her. She lives in the big guest room. She's very shy. Charlene, this is my daughter, Corinne. I'm ashamed to admit it, but I still don't know the names of my grandchildren. I met them for the first time today!"

"Oh Dad, I'm sorry! This is Hope, she's going to be a freshman this fall, and this is Tim. He's going into seventh grade." They are really good kids. They have been through a lot. They have been very resilient. I'm so proud of them. They never complain and they are a big help to me. They've had to be more or less self-sufficient since they were very young."

Hope and Tim, sensing their mother's unease clustered closer. They were the new kids again and were nervous. Their mother was nervous too, so the atmosphere was even more charged for them. The instability of their lives showed loud and clear.

"Hey, you guys are home now. You are here for as long as you want to be. After dinner, I'll give you the twenty-five-cent tour of this mausoleum. I hope you will find a way of making it your home."

"I really don't think that we have a real choice anymore. We're homeless and broke. I have fourteen cents. We had a hotdog each since yesterday. There was nothing in our refrigerator when we left Knoxville."

"Wow, that bad? "

"Yeah, twenty-five hours a week at Wal Mart, fifteen hours a week at KFC, and eighteen hours with Maids to Order, all at minimum wage. There were no benefits."

32 Father Bob's Dream

The little church was full. It was raining. There were oil lamps on stands here and there and two chandeliers with oil lamps hung from the ceiling. They were all lit because of the gloom outside. It was early spring because the trees were bare. The air had a chill to it. There was a pervasive feeling of love and togetherness- unity in the congregation. It was a palpable feeling. Everyone was dressed in their best clothes. As he walked up the aisle, he felt vaguely out of place. The building was new. The clothing was late eighteenth century-early nineteenth century. He was wearing his normal clericals, an Alb over a cassock with the stole for lent. A brass cross and two brass candlesticks graced the altar. The Common Book and the Bible were on the lectern in front of the altar. The congregation was singing in an unfamiliar language. The altar was against the wall. He took his place in front of the altar and started the mass. The familiar words of the mass came out of his mouth in the language of the congregation. It was the same mass he had celebrated on two continents in three languages. This new language came just as easily as English or Latin. As he celebrated the Mass, he felt a feeling of ease and unity with the congregation. As he invoked the Holy Spirit into the Host, A wave of warmth and love moved through him and the congregation, and he could see into the hearts of everyone in the building. It evoked the feeling that drew him into missionary work as a teenager. He felt totally welcomed.

"Robert", said a voice in the back of his mind, "I have brought you here to see what was and what you need to return here."

"I am your servant!"

"You must include everybody without judgement or criticism. I came for everybody, not just the few." "Everybody?"

"There will be people that tax your

understanding that will ask your counsel. Do not turn them away. They are as I have made them, as they have lessons to teach and learn. They are in your path for a reason. Do not question your faith in Me. It is strong enough. I have chosen you for this Mission for a reason. Don't question it. It's all about context. You need to look through it and minister to the souls inside. These people are my Faithful too. Only sixteen of them survived the next two years. They were branded heathen savages, but as you can see, they were faithful to Me. I loved them. They loved Me. Hate killed them. Hate is a product of ignorance, greed and laziness. To fight it requires love and knowledge with the hard work of spreading the knowledge that through love, all are saved. You must continue reaching out, even when things look hopeless. You are my faithful servant, and I am proud of you. Remember these people and spread the True Gospel that comes from the heart through love and prayer that you write through your life of faith, love, and prayer, and not the itinerary of others. Each of us writes his or her own Gospel. There is no room for hate in it. There is no room for prejudice in it. We must work together to bring about the Kingdom, not on Earth or government, but inside, where it counts- a Kingdom where love and peace reign together over everyone. You have the key to it in your heart. Open the door."

He awoke in the tiny confessional. It was a hot summer Saturday. The ink in his ballpoint had made a huge blot on his crossword puzzle. He was soaked in sweat. Somewhere in the woodwork, a dirt dauber wasp was working on her nest. The birds outside were claiming their territory.

33 Unole's Dreamcatcher

They marched through the countryside. Men on horses carrying rifles rode on the flanks of the column of humanity. The men on the horses were cursing at the people on the ground to move faster. The very old and the very young struggled to keep up. It was cold. There was a coating of fresh snow on the ground. Only a few of the people in the column had any winter clothing. He never remembered being so hungry. His feet hurt. They had been marching like that for weeks now on stale bread and salt pork with a thin gruel once a day. His mother was stumbling. She had a heavy cough. It had been with her for a whole week. She was very pale. Yesterday, she had fallen and one of the men on horseback had kicked her until she got back up and started walking again. Last week his best friend had tried to run away. He was shot dead and left where he landed as they marched on.

Unole woke with a start. The dream hung on her soul. She cried. She walked over to where Jack and Maryann slept and climbed between them. Maryanne woke up and saw the distress on her face.

"You had thet dream agin?"

"Yes Mama "

"Y'all's safe now. There's no soldiers here."

"But they's commin to git us, I knows it!"

"Not now, Chile, not now."

"The dream keeps commin back"

"Uncle Francis knows about these things, Y'all kin ask him."

The chill of early autumn was in the air. Maryanne and Unole were walking to the diner. Maryanne was going there to talk about going back to work. She had dressed up for the occasion. She was wearing a calico dress and a sweater. She was carrying a pair of heels and had a pair of pantyhose in her pocketbook. Unole was wearing a tear dress. It was the only dress she would wear. It was a simple garment. It was undyed unbleached raw cotton. The piece of fabric was folded in half. A slot was torn along the fold with another tear in the front to make a neck line. The torn edges were hemmed. It was stitched at the sides up to the arm holes. The bottom was hemmed. It was secured at the waist with a piece of wide ribbon. It had come to her in a dream. She only wore it when her mother demanded it of her. The rest of the time she wore a loincloth secured with a piece of clothesline. Unole was carrying a pair of black patent leather Maryjanes. They had been on her feet once at the shoe department at

Iggy's. It had taken an hour of persuasion from three people to get her to put them on her feet to try them on. They were the only shoes she owned. She had a pair of white ankle socks tucked under the ribbon at her waist. They were unworn, fresh out of the package. They were singing songs and laughing as they walked. Unole's hair was tied back into a ponytail with a piece of rawhide. Maryanne had tried to talk her into wearing a ribbon, but Unole had won the debate. Unole had wanted braids, but Maryanne wasn't up to the struggle of untangling her hair enough to divide it and braid it. Her red hair was thick and curly and always had foreign objects buried in it. Combing it out to braid it was a long-term project. Shortly after they reached the paved county road, a spike buck jumped out of the roadside thicket and ran across the road in front of them. As it bounded across the hayfield, Maryanne and Unole stared after it in awe and wonder. The noise of the deer bolting from the thicket startled them. Unole dropped a shoe. Their hearts raced as they watched the deer bound into the woods. Unole picked up her shoe and laughed. Maryanne looked down at her laughing child and smiled. The dream had faded into the past and Unole was back in now.

They arrived at the diner and went directly into the lady's room. As Maryanne pulled on her pantyhose and straightened them she said," Now Unole, y'all gots to wear them shoes. Y'all's not allowed to be in there without shoes."

"Yes Mama."

Covenant Roman Catholic Church

She dutifully pulled on her socks and struggled into her shoes. The smooth soles were not comfortable to her on the slippery tile floor of the rest room. She held onto her mother's skirt as they emerged from the restroom. It was lunch time and the diner was busy. Francis was sitting at his usual table eating a hamburger and doing paperwork. Unole saw him and ran to him.

"Uncle Francis!" she squealed, "we seed a deer!"

She climbed into his lap and hugged him.

"It ran real close to us!"

"Did it have antlers?"

"He was a spike"

"It's always a good sign when you see a buck when you ain't hunting them. How's my little warrior today?"

"I's good"

"You're growing up so fast. It seems like yesterday you were just a baby. Now you are a young lady."

"I don't want to be a lady. I's a warrior. I hunts!"

"I know, I've watched you."

"I got a rabbit yesterday. Mama cooked him for us."

"How did you get a rabbit?"

"I jumped on him."

"You jumped on a rabbit?"

"I watched him, and got closer and closer. If he moved at all, I stopped and waited. I got closer, then I jumped on him and squished him."

"You squished a rabbit."

"Yes sir, then I took him in to Mama to cook 'cause she won't let me eat rabbits raw."

Francis laughed and hugged her.

"You can get real sick eating raw rabbits. Your mama is right."

"I eats mice and birds raw."

"Birds?"

"They is hard to ketch! "

"You really shouldn't be eating them raw either. What do you do about the feathers?"

"I pulls the bigguns off, then I eats it."

Francis shook his head and smiled. This child had really strong medicine, and she wasn't three yet. He knew the circumstances of her conception and birth. The hilltop by the twin rocks was still bare of vegetation. It was a strong omen. The old ones foretold the coming of a prophet. She could talk now, He had to ask. He asked the question in Cherokee.

"Unole, tell me about your dreams."

"They're very sad. Our people are being herded like cattle to a place far away. There is snow and ice on our trail. There is much sadness and death. The soldiers are cruel."

"In the dreams, are you a girl?"

"No, I'm a boy, just making hair between my legs."

Francis was stunned. Her Cherokee was better than his. She spoke with the accent of the old ones. She was talking about the trail of tears in the 1830's. She was reliving it in her dreams. She had the culture inside of her. He had to teach her how to relieve the pain and turn the dreams in the right direction. The past was a foundation. Modern three-year-olds don't normally speak Cherokee. Of that he was certain.

"Do you want new dreams?"

"Yes. I walk that trail too much. It hurts me inside."

"You need to make a dreamcatcher. You have to make it yourself. You have to gather the makings yourself too. You have to do it alone. You have to think about the dreams while you make it. You need to sing your own song. It's in your heart. You need to let it come out in whatever tongue it comes in."

"I had one before the soldiers came."

"In the dream?"

"Yes. I made it myself."

"You need to make one for here and now. The lost one won't help here."

33 Family Dinner

For the first time in years, the dining room table had people eating at it. The kitchen table was too small for the group now. It was the first time that everyone had eaten in a group. Charlene and Louie prepared the meal. The task was complicated by the fact that the three occupants of the big house had different eating schedules and everything was single serve microwavable items. Eating together as a group was never tried, and now the group was six. There is no supermarket in Sterling forks. There is a 7/11. Huntsville or Lynchburg are the choices for a major grocery shopping expedition. The three new arrivals were a surprise. They were hungry. Charlene and Louie went to work. Microwave meals were broken down to their component parts. Entrees were separated from sides. The preparations generated a frightening quantity of trash. The hardest part was integrating the mashed potatoes and separating the gravy from them to make them appetizing in a family style setting. It had to be family style. It was a celebration of family. Using the china was discussed. The everyday dishes were chosen instead because it was to mark the beginning of everyday life for a family that had been fragmented but was now back together. Fine china would be too stressful. The flatware was everyday stainless too. The silver service remained securely locked away. It would be too much trouble to polish it anyway in the timeframe needed to assemble the modest family dinner. It was the first-time Corinne had sat at that table since the exchange with her mother about her new boyfriend, half way through eleventh grade. She had stormed away from the table and out of the house with just the clothes on her back and her pocketbook, never to return or write. When she visited her father in the hospital, she hadn't stopped by the house. She stayed with a high school friend in town. Now, she was sitting at the same table with her children and three strangers. Even the person she "knew" was a stranger to her as everything had changed. This nice lady was her father. The idea itself made her head swim. The face was the same, but it was wearing makeup and attached to an obviously female body wearing female clothing. The other nice lady was about her age and looked like her mother, but was kind and non-judgmental, and as a bonus, sober. Then there was the strange little man. He seemed nice. He was younger than she was. There was something about the way he moved that just wasn't right to her. He didn't have the local accent. He talked like the younger lady who also didn't have the local accent. She couldn't place the accent, familiar as it seemed. Conversation was subdued. After Charlene said Grace, everyone ate. The kids were starved. Hope didn't even try to act like a lady. She ate like a refugee from a third world country. Tim simply guarded his plate and shoveled the food in. Corinne sat and tried to figure out the strangers in her childhood home. All three of them made her nervous. The only one she could even relate to was the older woman who claimed to be her dad. She did look like him but dads are supposed to be men. This one was definitely a woman. She was wearing one of Mom's wigs. She remembered being with her in Nashville when she bought it. When she talked, though, she sounded like Dad. Her head swam. The younger lady, seemed nervous. She didn't say much. She moved around and made sure everyone got enough to eat.

Tim broke the silence. "How can you be Grandpa, when you are a lady?"

"Cancer."

"I never saw cancer turn someone into a lady before."

"Neither did I, until it happened to me."

"Then you are Grandpa."

"Yes, but something happened that made me into a lady. Have you had Sex Education yet?"

Covenant Roman Catholic Church

"They don't teach it in our county."

"Shit, I'll have to start from scratch then."

"What do you mean by that?"

"You need to know about how the male reproductive system works and the parts of it."

"It's simple. We have a dick and a pair of balls."

"Right, but we have another part deep inside called the prostate. That is where I got the cancer."

"I have heard about prostate cancer on TV, but how can prostate cancer turn you into a lady?"

"I didn't see a doctor until I couldn't pee at all and got sick from it."

"Why didn't you see a doctor when it was hard to pee at first?"

"I was working."

"Working?"

Covenant Roman Catholic Church

"I traveled all over the world and lived in hotels. There never seemed to be time to see a doctor. The cancer took my prostate, the inner part on the urethra and the ball end of my penis. All they could save was the outer urethra which they stitched to what was left of my bladder. They had to do a bone graft on my pelvis. I lost a big piece of my pubic arch. They gave me a vagina to attach a fake penis to, so I would look normal in rest rooms and locker rooms. It didn't work right, so the vagina closed up so I couldn't use the prosthesis anymore. Do you know what hormones are?"

"Not really. People talk about them raging and stuff and how they make you crazy sometimes."

My cancer is testosterone triggered. In the presence of testosterone, it grows like crazy. They cut off my balls to stop the production of testosterone. Everyone's body make hormones of both sexes. Because I'm not making testosterone any more, estrogen, the female hormone took over. Because of the cancer meds, the adrenal glands on top of my kidneys started making a lot of it. I started feminizing. My body fat moved around to different places and I started growing tits. I never intended it to happen, but it did. I tried to stay a man for as long as I could. Airport security is what made me give up and be a lady."

"How can airport security do that?"

"My passport and driver's license no longer match my body. I have tits and a vagina."

With that, Corinne and Tim both started laughing hysterically at the irony of it. Hope looked up from her plate and grinned. Grandpa was indeed a lady and came by it honestly. Ben, AKA Mom, AKA Thelma took a bow. The tension was broken and they were family.

"I still have to talk to my lawyer and accountant to fix the paperwork. Benjamin is not a good name for a lady."

34 Mike Foster

Mike Foster grew up in the shack in the woods. He married a woman from town named Doris. He was a whiskey maker by trade. He grew his corn using traditional Cherokee farming methods. He only disturbed enough top cover to plant his hills of the three sisters, corn, squash, and beans. He lived off the land. Like the other Fosters in the area he was a descendant of Bear Claw, a straggler from the great uprooting. He spoke, read, and wrote Cherokee. When his son Jack was fifteen, Doris passed away. It was a painful lingering death from M.S. He spent every waking moment not involved in securing food, tending to her. They met in elementary school. They were fourteen when they eloped to the shack. Mike's parents welcomed her with open arms they were sixteen when Jack was born. They were happy in the shack in the woods. Mike was twenty-one when his parents passed. His dad was Cherokee, and his mother was Chickasaw, from Trail's End in

Oklahoma. They spoke Cherokee in the home. Mike's dad was Francis the Toad Smasher's brother. Mike was so distraught at the loss of Doris; he couldn't live in the shack anymore. He moved into the woods off a U.S. Forest Service access trail. He built a lodge from traditional materials. It was warm and comfortable. The only human contact he had was his son, Jack and the man from Huntsville that bought his whiskey. Everything he used came from the land except ammo for his rifle and shotgun. Jack brought it in from town for him.

Mike made sour mash. He aged it in Jack Daniels barrels. He shipped it at three years. It felt and tasted like scotch. His still was stainless steel with a copper water jacketed condenser. It ran a fifty-gallon batch. It burned wood. It was a column unit. He ran the batch through it three times so that the resultant whiskey was about one hundred and ninety proof. He then put it in barrels to age. He was working about thirty acres for corn to make it. It was

301

all done by hand. The little patch of creek bottom produced fine corn. The only concession to modernity was the old WPA maintenance shop on the creek bank that housed his still and support for it. There was a turbine in the creek that powered an overhead shaft that ran a corn sheller, a feed grinder and a cordwood saw. His mash tubs were red oak tanks bound with birch bands. He built them in place. The technology of the tubs was pure Cherokee. The only concession to modernity there was steel tools for shaping the wood. Jack had spent time working in the distillery, but it was not what he wanted to do. He simply didn't like whiskey. He didn't like the taste. He didn't like the smell. He didn't like the high he got from it. He was making great money selling pot to the college students. He didn't have to bust his ass doing it. It meant walking to Knoxville every so often, but it was well worth his while, and the path he took to Knoxville was through territory that didn't see many travelers, so he was welcomed with open arms by the people that lived there. There were quite a few of them. The narcotics people never looked for a kid walking through the woods with a backpack. He always stopped in on his dad when he went to, and from Knoxville. It was a three day walk each way to Knoxville. Mike worried every trip. The national forest is huge, steep, and lightly traveled in most places. In that forest, there are places where taking a mule through would be cruelty to animals. It was peaceful and calm there. Mike kept himself busy and made first rate whiskey.

It had been years since Doris passed away. He missed her terribly. Her spirit was alive in the woods. She was buried in the ancient burial ground that his ancestors had used since before the Spanish moved into Georgia. It wasn't far from his still. He didn't want to go too far away from it. He would visit with Jack when he came through. Jack missed her too. They would sit in the burial ground and smoke. They would make offering to the ancestors and leave.

They always felt refreshed afterwards. Today, Mike was excited. Jack was bringing Maryanne and Unole along to visit. Maryanne knew Doris and loved her. Doris loved Maryanne too and hinted about marriage. Then she was gone. She didn't travel to the burial ground very often, because she didn't like walking back alone, as Jack was usually on his way to Knoxville when he passed through. Today was different. It was a family trip. It was time for Unole to meet her grandfather. Mike was excited. Jack had told him stories about her. He wanted to be with this amazing child. He talked to the spirit of Doris. "Doris, my love, they are coming to see us!" The wind rustled in the trees as if to answer him. He heard voices on the access road. His pulse raced. His family was here. He hadn't felt this joyful for a long time. He too loved Maryanne. She was English, but she was of the land too. She spoke a little Cherokee, but preferred English, at least her version of it. She loved him too. She liked his gentle way and his dedication to the Land. When Doris died, she understood why he disappeared into the woods. The forest healed his hurt and feeling of loss. He couldn't live in the shack anymore, because there was too much of Doris's final illness there. He moved into the still house until he built his lodge. Maryanne loved the simplicity of the lodge. She felt strangely at home there. It was a traditional Cherokee longhouse, with the hearth in the middle of the living area. A raised area was around the hearth with a narrow break in it for bringing in firewood, food, and other things that needed fire. It was made out of traditional materials and decorated with traditional artwork. The only concession to modern times was the addition of electric light from a generator running off the turbine in the creek. That and a couple of modern rifles. Just about every soft surface was made of some form of deer skin or another. It was cozy inside. It was also quiet. It was built with love and dedication. There were no totally plane surfaces nor sharp corners. It was organic in shape.

Unole greeted Mike in Cherokee. Mike was surprised and returned the greeting also in Cherokee. They talked about the trip through the forest and the things she saw on the way. Except for the inevitable small child accent and difficulty with certain sounds, her command of the language was excellent. Mike was impressed. Her command of the language amazed him. His mother who had grown up at Trail's End in Oklahoma didn't speak it that well. It felt good to Mike to be speaking the language again. Since Doris passed away, he didn't have the opportunity to speak it much. His granddaughter spoke it better than she

Covenant Roman Catholic Church

spoke English, and she spoke it well for a three-year-old. But then, her English wasn't exactly English. It was pure Rocky Top.

Unole had replaced the piece of clothesline securing her loincloth with a band of rawhide she had frayed the ends out into a fringe and placed beads on the end of each strand of the fringe. Looking at her, he wasn't sure if he could determine the gender of the child, as the loincloth was her only garment. Thinking back on the traditions, he knew that Unole had chosen her gender role, and it wasn't totally female. It wasn't female at all. His granddaughter was a rare child of two spirits. She had a female body, but the soul of a warrior. He could see it in her eyes. He could see it in the way she held herself and moved. He was awed and scared at the same time. After visiting with

Unole for a while more he pulled Jack aside.

"Jack, there is no way that child will function in the schools here. She will end up killing someone."

"I know. She doesn't conform to a modern American child at all, much less a girl."

"She hits the school; she will attract bullies."

"I know. Children can be cruel."

"She has red hair, and probably a temper to match. Somebody picks on her, it will cause an explosion. She's strong enough and fast enough to really hurt someone."

"I get where you are going with this. We are going to have to home school her until she's old enough to go to Trail's End."

"I'll foot the bill for Trail's end when she's old enough."

"Uncle Francis made the same offer."

Both men realized that Unole was indeed a cyclone ripping through both cultures. The Cherokee culture wouldn't be the same either. Here indeed was the prophet foretold by the Ojibwa. A mutual shiver ran through them. They had their work cut out for them. They also knew that they had a lot to learn.

35 Deidre's Homecoming

In Memphis, Deidre blossomed as a figure in the Beale St social scene. She was married to a successful saxophonist. He was almost twenty years older than she was, but they were more or less happy. She spent a lot of time in the studio and in the various clubs around Memphis with an occasional foray into Nashville, New York, and LA. She wore designer clothing and fine jewelry. They had a daughter together, but she died of an aneurism at twelve. She had lingered in a chronic vegetative state for about a year, and then was gone without ever regaining consciousness. Deidre was broken by it emotionally as was her husband. The show had to go on, but the death of their daughter hovered in the background. The marriage got loveless because of the guilt and sadness and her husband's growing impotence from prostate issues. Both of them drank and snorted cocaine, so there was very little cushion for rainy days. They projected am image of success, but the truth be told, they had nothing. They lived in a furnished apartment above a club on Beale St It was a third-floor walk-up in the back of the building. Diedre's husband was a passionate man. It showed in his music. He played the entire range of saxophones. When he practiced in the apartment, it transported Deidre to a safe and wondrous place. She liked the bass sax best. The notes in the low register went to the core of her being. He was fast and accurate in his fingering and conveyed tremendous emotion through it. She lived to hear him play. She put up with drunkenness, abuse, and infidelity just to bask in the sound of his music. She treated the pain of neglect with alcohol and cocaine, sometimes separately, sometimes together. She was hooked on coke, but it was always around, so she really didn't care about it. He was hooked on coke too, so as long as he got gigs, there would be coke around. He covered all the big names of the twentieth century and had a pretty good catalogue of his own. His work on the soprano sax was his living. He was the best local interpreter of John Coltrane. His work reflected the passion he had for that catalogue. Coltrane's estate opened the catalogue to him and he picked it up and ran with it. Deidre loved watching his quartet play in the local clubs. She loved the way he interacted with the audience and the way he would totally lose himself in the music. From the outside, people would think that the couple had it all. In private, when the music wasn't playing, it was a world of chaos and violence. Deidre always had a bruise somewhere on her face or body. Sometimes she wondered why she was staying there. The scene was seductive, and the cocaine took away the pain, so she stayed. People envied her. She was small, slender and moved well. She was good at hiding her shy and submissive nature, by dressing well and making casual conversation. In reality, she didn't have a friend in the world, as she was desperately afraid of commitment since their daughter died.

One Saturday night, while playing a Coltrane infused bebop version of Gershwin's summertime on the soprano sax, her husband had a massive stroke and dropped dead on the stage. Suddenly she was alone. She was numb through the wake and funeral. There wasn't enough money for a grave and monument, so she had him cremated. She scattered his ashes along Beale St., where he had spent most of his life. She counted sixteen ex-girlfriends at the funeral. All the music magazines ran worshipful obituaries for him and there was even a small piece in Time. She found herself in a small walk-up full of saxophones and sheet music. He didn't leave a will because he was too busy and too stoned to think about it. There were a few royalties from the label, but not much else besides her wardrobe and jewelry. She had a three hundred dollar a day cocaine addiction. She sold a couple of bracelets and checked in to rehab. She did it because she didn't like what she saw in the mirror after the funeral. She was at the limit of what makeup would hide. Before she left for the Betty Ford Clinic, she put everything into storage and put it on automatic payment. There wasn't enough to fill a small storage bay. Except for the clothing, none of it really appropriate for daily or long term use, there was really nothing to show for the years on Beale St. There were a few photos of their daughter and the jewelry. Of the jewelry, very little of it had much beyond sentimental value. While in Betty Ford, she pondered that state of affairs. She had no marketable skills. She could barely make coffee. She was a terrible housekeeper. She was totally ignorant of finances. Her husband handled that. She didn't even drive. She never learned how. Her husband's agent/ manager set up a trust fund for her. It paid out a monthly stipend that still left her eligible for food stamps and Medicaid. She had no work history and didn't even have a Social Security number, as she never had any money in her name until the trust fund was set up in her name by the Agent/ Manager. There was only one alternative, after Betty Ford. It was to crawl home to Sterling Forks. Maybe Dad would take her in. She hadn't had contact with the family since before her mother's funeral. The last contact was acrimonious and she still had a warrant out for her arrest on various drug related charges as well as an aiding and abetting charge stemming from a high school relationship. She had to leave town before the funeral because someone called the cops during a scene in the hospital with her siblings. There was still no alternative. She had to try going back home. She didn't have enough clothing to need a suitcase. She had bus fare, just barely, if she didn't eat anything on the way.

Covenant Roman Catholic Church

The bus trip from Betty Ford to Sterling Forks was a marathon ride. She panhandled a burger in Omaha. She drank out of the water fountains in the bus stations on layovers and slept on the bus. She had to walk from the bus station in sterling Forks to the big house, because she couldn't afford the fare on the local bus to the suburbs. She didn't want to attract attention by panhandling. It was bad enough in Omaha where nobody knew her family. In Sterling Forks, she was Miranda's perfect younger daughter. It was too much for her to handle to try. There was just too much shame. She walked. About a mile into her hike to the big house, one of her shoes disintegrated. Like all the other shoes she owned over the years, they were more for looks than for function. The walk from the bus station was beyond the design limit for an Italian designed cork wedge. The straps securing the wedge to

Covenant Roman Catholic Church

her foot separated from the cork section of the wedge, leaving her suddenly and unevenly barefoot. She tossed the shoes into the weeds on the roadside in disgust. The pavement was hot on her feet as she trudged on. It was ten at night when she finally reached the front door of the house. It looked pretty much the same as it did when she left it. With great trepidation, she rang the doorbell. A long time passed. She rang it again. A short youngish man answered the door.

36 Father Bob Shanghais Charlene

Mass had let out. Father Bob stood at the doorway of the little white church and greeted his flock. As Charlene walked by, He grabbed her elbow.

"Charlene, I need a favor from you."

"What would it be, Father?"

"Do you have unquestioned access to that car?"

"I don't know, I never asked."

"Fred Katz and I need a ride to Birmingham to a Jesuit convocation and retreat. He is a guest speaker."

Charlene laughed. "He's not a Jesuit, father, He's a Jew."

"That's why he's a guest speaker, because he is a Jew. He has some interesting insights on our Faith."

Covenant Roman Catholic Church

"How can a Jew who, is marginally observant at best, provide insights to a group of Jesuits."

"Very simple: Jesus was a Jew. Fred speaks the same language, and prays in it. He calls it arguing with God, but in the true definition of prayer, it's prayer. Scripture shows Jesus in the Garden arguing with God. It's the same thing. As Catholics, we have lost that gift. Most of us only pray under duress, or when we want something. We aren't carrying on the dialog that is needed for true communion with God. He came to Mass with Marjorie, one Sunday and we talked afterward. He gave me the actual words in the actual language that were spoken during the Last Supper. Since then I have opened doors in my faith that I wasn't even aware of."

"How So?"

"The Jews have, since the fall of Herod's Temple, have been sojourners in other peoples' lands. They have practiced their faith and traditions wherever they ended up. "

"What does that have to do with the Jesuits?

"Like the Jews in the world, we Jesuits are an island in the Catholic Church. Occasionally, we're persecuted, but we have our faith and traditions, pretty much unchanged from the beginning. We are scattered throughout the world, doing the heavy lifting of the Church, but not getting much credit for it. We follow the original mandate, and spread the good news, The Jews are also following an original mandate, given to Abraham and codified through Moses. Over millennia, they have survived with their faith and tradition, more or less intact. It's all about getting back to our roots. Like Jesus, we Jesuits are fighting the secular organization that has grown up around

our faith. Like it or not, Christianity is a sect of
Judaism. We believe in, and worship the same God.
We have the same basic Mandate, given to
Abraham. We need to get back to it, with our
mandate added to it. They are not incompatible. It's
the same basic road."

"Wow, I never looked at it that way."

"What Catholic has? Here, in the
Bible belt, I have learned what it's like to be a Jew
in a Christian world. Because I am a Catholic, I am
viewed with a certain amount of suspicion by the
other faith groups, even though we are all
Christians. I've learned a lot here. As a Jesuit, I am
viewed with the same suspicion in the Church
Hierarchy. The powers that be in the Church would
rather see us gone, even though we run a lot of
mission churches."

"Yes, I have seen some of it myself, as a
Catholic in the Bible belt. People are constantly
trying to reform me. They want me to be born again,

even though I have been baptized and confirmed.
When I came to work here, I was worried that there
would be no Catholic Church in town. I was
delighted to find one. You have been truly a light in
the darkness."

"As a priest, I too have struggled here. The
secular world is strong. It's seductive. I was
experiencing a dark time in my faith when you and
Marjorie walked into my confessional. I was
looking at the small size of my congregation,
compared to the others in town. I looked at my little
hand me down building and my reception by the
faith community in town, and was getting to think,
"What's the use of my being here?" I am not
converting heathens to the faith. I am just a simple
priest in a little church in the middle of nowhere.
Then you two walked into my life carrying a
monstrous sin. It impacted me as a priest and as a
man. I was struck dumb by the enormity of it. As a
priest, I sensed your pain. It was so hard to deal with

it, because nobody avails themselves to the sacrament anymore. I wasn't ready. I could feel the pain in Marjorie's voice as she told me what she had done. I could feel her genuine sorrow for it and her repentance. I couldn't speak. I could feel the blackness of evil and revulsion go through my being. It was visceral. The words of our savior, as quoted in scripture came to me as to what was required of me. I couldn't act. I couldn't even speak. My heart was breaking from the weight of my responsibilities as priest and upholder of morals. They were in direct conflict as how I felt as a man, representing men. I had gone back into active Ministry because I was addicted to the rush of the Holy Spirit going through me during the Invocation. I hadn't been finding it lately and I felt abandoned. I could have continued doing the circuit of churches doing fundraising and outreach for the rest of my life. It was offered to me, but I felt a need to be a priest. Here in this backwater, I wasn't officiating

over weddings. I wasn't baptizing people. I wasn't
confirming very many people. I wasn't even doing
Last Rites. I was just another preacher that everyone
in town called Padre. I was frustrated and depressed.
I had to be a real agent of the Lord and Savior, but
when I was really needed I wasn't ready. An
amazing thing happened. The Holy Spirit came to
me and took over. It was the strongest thing I have
ever felt. I was a leaf in a cyclone, being swept
through a storm. When I came back down, I still had
to hear your confession. I am so grateful to both of
you for restoring my faith in myself and my Lord
and Savior."

"We did that?"

"Yes, you did that. Then Marjorie wasn't
finished with me. She introduced me to Fred Katz.
She first gave me a copy of his second book. She
told me to read it. I did. After a respectful period,
she brought him to mass. I didn't realize that the
book hadn't been distributed yet, and that that was

an advance copy. I found a fundamental truth in it. My trail was just as bloody and destructive as anyone else's. I had sown hurt and anguish through my life too. I needed a way to atone for it. I couldn't find one here. I am still needed here as a priest. There is nobody to replace me. I expressed my feelings to my superiors as well as my recent experiences in faith and sent the book along as well as some of the things we had talked about in conversation. I expressed our mutual feelings of isolation and loneliness. That book traveled. They couldn't find other copies. They tried."

Covenant Roman Catholic Church

"I have some bad news for you. The publisher out of spite and anger at Fred for missing deadlines stuck the entire first printing in a warehouse in Chicago. They didn't distribute it through normal channels, but instead sold them to a marginal dealer, also in Chicago at a deeply discounted price, and then wrote Fred a check for the royalty. There won't be any more copies available as Fred signed away the rights. Not only that, but his agent abandoned him as well as his publisher. He has been effectively blackballed."

"That's terrible. He has a gift that must be shared. I read his first book after his second one and found a great amount of pure humanity in it. I want more!"

"Can you do it for me?

"Do what?'

"Give us a ride."

Covenant Roman Catholic Church

"Oh, yeah, a ride! I don't know. I never asked except for an occasional errand. I almost didn't transfer my license. I walked everywhere. I'll ask Ben. By the way, did you hear what happened?"

"Vaguely. I hear he's now she and calling herself Thelma."

"I'll try to get the car."

37 Sid's Redemption

Sid heard footsteps in his cell block. It didn't happen very often except at mealtimes. It wasn't mealtime, and the shoes didn't sound like the trustee that brought his meal. He heard the bolt on his cell door release and the door slide open. A guard appeared in the doorway. He was smiling. None of it added up.

"The warden wants to see you."

"Oh?"

"Do what you need to, to get ready, it's going to be vertical for a while, so you need to hydrate as good as possible."

"Any idea about what it's about?"

"Not really, but he seemed happy when I talked to him."

Sid turned a depend inside out and stuffed it into his orifice. He put on another and changed into a clean modified jumpsuit. He drank three glasses of water and went with the guard.

The warden was smiling when Sid walked into the office. He had never seen that before.

"Sid, I have great news for you."

"Am I getting out?"

"No, but it will make your life here much more comfortable."

"How so?"

"The doctors at Vanderbilt figured out a way of making you hold your contents better so you don't drip any more, and so you can live with other people here. We need your cellblock, so Corrections is OK with footing the bill."

"What are they going to do?"

"They are going to sew your orifice shut and perform an ostomy so you have a bag on your side to collect your shit and they are going to make you a new urethra so that you can urinate normally, or at least have a catheter. It's a longshot, but the GI team, the urology team, and the plastic surgery team have figured it out. It's about a $200,000.00 procedure."

Covenant Roman Catholic Church

"They're going to fix me" Sid broke down in tears.

"Yes, they are. You survived here like that for three years. We didn't figure on even a year the way you were when you came here. It was a matter of money on a hopeless convict. Your work with scared straight made Time and Newsweek. The national media is aware of your condition and the fact that you occupy an entire cellblock. Your condition is an embarrassment to the State. Your suffering has caught the eye of the media, and people are clamoring for us to do something about it."

"When is this going to happen?"

"Next week."

"Next week?"

"You're going to Nashville!"

Covenant Roman Catholic Church

Sid was stunned. He was totally speechless. He didn't expect anyone to care about his plight. He brought it on himself. Now somebody decided that he had suffered enough. He was overcome with mixed emotions. He wanted to shout with joy but he wanted to cry too. He stood in the warden's office and tried to process the news. He was getting fixed, at least as well as a man with no pelvic floor can be fixed. Three years ago, the same doctors shook their heads and said, Sid, you're fucked. We've got nothing for you. There is too much missing. Sid had never experienced joy. He couldn't process it. He broke down and cried. The warden, embarrassed, looked away.

A week later Sid was in the ice cream truck sitting on unpainted aluminum riding down I 40 to Nashville. The truck was set up for twelve inmates, but Sid was riding alone. There was nobody on the other side of the partition. His sore behind was pounded by the expansion joints in the pavement. He'd stuffed an inside out depend in the orifice and put another one over it, but he was still leaking and his skin was burning from the digestive juices. The aluminum was getting slippery. When they took a sharp turn, he had trouble staying in place. Still, he was glad he was on this trip. All that would be gone. He would be housebroken! Now there was a word, housebroken. He had been shitting on the floor like a pet bird for over three years, now he could live with people, because he was housebroken. He laughed out loud, then caught himself. There was nobody to share it with. He hadn't had a bunkmate since he got off on the home invasion charge. He had no one. He was alone. Maybe if he was housebroken he could have someone to talk to. It would be nice to have a Bunkie again, even though they were usually a disaster for him. Maybe after the experiences of the past several years, he could tolerate somebody sharing space with him. It would be hard, but the

last three years in solitary confinement taught him
that he needed people in his life. He could change.
He wasn't angry anymore. It had burned out of him
on the hillside in the park. Who would tolerate him
though? He dozed off as the ice cream truck
bounced over the interstate.

The dream of home didn't come this time. It
was a deep dreamless sleep. The backup alarm woke
him as the ice cream truck backed into the
ambulance entrance at Vanderbilt Hospital. His
shackles were released from the bench and the door
opened. The driver and a guard motioned him to
climb out. His shackles were removed and thrown
back into their place in the truck. A leather restraint
took the place of the handcuffs and he was led into
triage. A friendly nurse took his vital signs and
information. She was surprised about his weight. He
was six feet tall but only weighed a hundred pounds.
They led him to a cubicle and took his soaked
modified from him and replaced it with a hospital

johnny. They removed the two soaked depends and put on a fresh one after inspecting him and cleaning him up. The guard gave him a glass of water. Soon a resident came in. He poked and prodded him and wrote on his chart, without saying a word to him. He pulled down the depend and looked at the rash on his behind, put the depend back and left. A nurse came in and rubbed a cream on the rash. Another resident came in and checked his eyes and ears, looked down his throat, palpated his neck, wrote on his chart and left. Nobody spoke to him. Soon an older doctor came in.   "Sid, I hope we've figured things out since you were here last time."

"I hope so too."

"What we are going to do, is borrow a piece of skin from the inside of your leg and fill the space where your pelvic floor used to be. We 're going to take a piece of your colon and make a urethra out of it and put it through in the appropriate place then we will take the rest of your colon and direct it through the side of your belly, just beside your naval. It's called an ostomy. You are lucky, because you still have a colon. The ostomy will narrow things so that the contents of your colon won't run out onto the floor anymore. You are going to have to be careful about what you eat and make sure that the pouch we will give you fills up regularly. If your feces gets too hard it will be painful coming out. You still won't have control of your bowel movements, but at least things will be contained. We don't know how well our urethra will work. As we've never done this before. You may have to spend the rest of your life with a catheter. We don't know for sure as you have only about an inch of your original urethra. Hopefully there's more, but we haven't looked inside yet. All we know is what we saw last time you were here."

"Anything will be an improvement, Doc."

The doctor took out a sharpie and put an X on his belly beside his naval.

"This is where we will put the ostomy."

"Who's going to change the bag for me? I don't see a nurse coming in to my cell every so often."

"You will. We will teach you before you leave here."

"You said something about a catheter."

"We don't know if you will have any bladder control, because when your prostate was removed with your pelvic floor, we don't know how much urethra was left or even if you have a valve anymore. Can you control when you urinate, can you feel an urgency when your bladder gets full and urinate, or does it just drip out?

"I never paid any attention to it. I think it just drips out, but I don't have any feeling there. Anyway. I can't tell."

"OK that means that the pelvic nerve is gone. There's nothing we can do about that. Maybe, you will have residual sensation at the base of your bladder. We have no idea about what exactly was done inside. We'll find out after you recover from the surgery."

The doctor shook Sid's hand and left. Another slightly younger doctor came in.

"We're going to steal some skin from the inside of your thigh to fill the gap where your pelvic floor used to be. We are going to pinch up a lump and force it to stretch for a few days so that when we remove it, it won't leave much of a scar. Lay back on the gurney and spread your legs...Eww, we're going to have to do something about all that inflammation before we operate."

He jotted something down on Sid's chart. Now let's see.... Yeah, about here. This isn't going to be easy. There's no fat layer here. You've lost a lot of weight since I saw you last time. I only need a five-inch strip about two inches wide."

"Ouch"

"I'm sorry, it's tight and inflamed.
It's going to be hard to pinch and stretch."

"That hurt!"

"I know, I'll
numb it up before I put the staples into it."

"Staples?"

"That is how I'm going to hold the
stretch for a week or so, until it holds its shape
enough to separate it from your thigh and sew it into
place where it is needed.

"You are going to
move skin around?"   "It's what
plastic surgery is all about. We do this with burn
victims and amputations all the time. The inner
thigh skin will be perfect for the tender area between
your legs. Except in your case, it's usually quite
loose and easy to pinch off and stretch for that
purpose. It also is easy to shape as it's smooth and

relatively thin. I wish we had more time to build up a fat layer to hold it in shape for stretching. I've written a prescription for the diaper rash you have. I need to clear that up so I can pinch up the skin. If I put staples there now, I could guarantee a staph infection. It's a salve."

"How are we going to stop the dripping?"

"As soon as we can book an OR, we are going to divert your colon to the ostomy. We are going to sew shut about a foot and a half of the descending colon temporarily to seal up your lower abdomen while we work on getting you ready for the rest of your reconstruction. Part of that will be to evaluate your urinary function. We need to see if you have any control of your bladder. I am the plastic surgeon that is going to reconstruct your crotch."

A nurse walked in with a tube of salve. She rubbed it on the rash and put a surgical drape across it secured with tape to protect it from the drip from his orifice. The edge of the tape went to the edges of the orifice, protecting the insides of both legs. The plastic surgeon and the nurse walked out together. All that activity made Sid tired. He dozed off. A nurse woke him for lunch. It was a clear chicken broth in a cup with a serving of lemon Jell-O. It was served on real dishes instead of a stainless-steel prison tray. That difference alone lifted Sid's spirits. It didn't matter about the food. It was all about the presentation. He wasn't inside the prison. He was outside the walls. He was interacting with people who were actually concerned about him. It felt good.

He noticed that the guard that had been hovering around since his arrival was gone. He figured that he had gone to lunch in the cafeteria. While he was pondering that, a nurse came in, cleaned him up, and changed the draping and re medicated him. When she was finished, the guard was still not to be seen. In fact, there were no security people anywhere. He was still restrained

somewhat, but he was no longer tied to the gurney

His restraints were an IV and a jungle of monitoring

wires. He wasn't going anywhere and everyone

knew it. He wanted this more than anything else in

his entire life. He would no longer be a hidden

sideshow freak. He would no longer scare teenagers.

He could finally figure out what it was to be human

among humans. He was grateful.

Another doctor came in with another nurse.

He had a Foley catheter and a sterile plastic

container. He took the container that he was

draining into and emptied it into the container, then

returned it to its place. Since the IV was started, the

flow had slowed to a drip. The nurse probed around

and found the stoma in his rectal wall. She inserted

the Foley and inflated the anchor. She then took a

sharpie and marked the area on the catheter where it

passed into the stoma. She hooked it to a bag and

hung it on the chassis of the gurney. She then left

the room. The doctor pulled on the Foley and checked the mark. He measured the catheter to the joint to the tube leading to the bag. He noted his measurements on the chart.

"Sid, I am the urologist that will hopefully enable you to pee normally. Over the next couple of days, after I get the samples I need, I am going to see how much bladder control you have. We are going to extend your urethra to the outside of your body. We will borrow tissue from your rectum and form a tube and graft it to the stump of your existing urethra."

"I can't feel anything there."

"What do you mean?"

"I haven't had the urge to pee since I woke up in the park."

"Not at all?

"Nope."

"I'm going to run some tests and see if I can fix you so you can pee. Worst case would be a catheter like the one we just put in. Even that would be better than the way you are now."

"Even death would be better, but I even screwed that up."

"If things go right, you won't want to die as badly. Tomorrow, I am going to do a bladder capacity test. I will use an ultrasound and inspect your bladder to see if you can sense when it's full. I think that it hasn't been full enough to tell you for a long time."

"It would be nice if I didn't drip all the time. I always have a headache and I'm always thirsty."

"Rest up, I'll see you in the morning."

For the first time in over three years, Sid's legs were dry. He reveled in the feeling. He was sleeping on cloth with a blanket and a pillow. He cherished the moment.

At six AM. a nurse came by and took his vital signs and changed the bag on the IV. She emptied the urine bag into a graduated container and recorded her reading. She checked for color and clarity and noted her findings on the chart.

"How're y'all feelin, Sid?"

"I've died and gone to heaven."

"No, serious, How Y'all feelin?"

"I feel great. The headache that I have lived with for three years is gone."

"Let me look at your rash."

"Knock yourself out. It feels a lot better."

"A couple more days the plastic surgeon can come and do his thing on your thigh. It's looking good."

"I'm nervous about the staples. What if they get infected before he can move the skin?"

"I won't let that happen. Nobody else will either. "

"I'm afraid."

"Afraid of the surgery?"

"No, I'm afraid I will end up unchanged, that it won't work. I couldn't live with that. I would rather die on the table."

"There are two hospitals in the South that can do this. This one, and Emory in Atlanta. We take pride in our ability to do the impossible and make it look commonplace."

"I'm still scared. This happened to me over three years ago. I've lost over eighty pounds. I'm malnourished and never took care of myself in the past. I grew up in the correctional system of Tennessee. I really don't think I'm a good risk."

"Look, Sid, your heart and lungs are good. Your blood pressure is perfect. You are still fairly young. The plastic guys are bitching about a fat layer, or rather no fat layer. You are a perfect risk. Besides, the national media is watching us."

Covenant Roman Catholic Church

Breakfast came. It was clear turkey broth and lime Jell-O. Sid drank the broth greedily. He was hungry. He ate the Jell-O and was still hungry. He paged the nurses' station. After about five minutes, a nurse came in.

"Is this all I'm getting for breakfast?"

"I'm afraid so, Sid, we need your gut to be clean and dry for the procedure, and we need the mess on your legs healed. Aren't you happy that you're dry?"

"Yeah, I could really like that feeling. It's nice not having to worry about keeping my digestive contents in."

"I might be able to get you another serving of broth at about ten. I'll ask the GI guys."

"Thanks. I really appreciate that."

A pair of orderlies came in and handed Sid a TV remote.

"We took up a collection. You are going to be here for a while and you didn't have money for the television service. We know how boring it is to be in a hospital. We hope you will enjoy it." Sid turned on the TV. He had a remote in his hand. For the first time in three years, he had control over what he saw on TV. He started to cry again.

"Thanks, guys. You have no idea how this makes me feel."

"We're here all the time. We've watched patients go crazy with boredom. We had to do something."

"It means the world to me. I can't put it into words."

"Just enjoy it"

Covenant Roman Catholic Church

In the prison, the TV was on 24/7 and always on the same channel. People usually give their dogs better programming than Sid was subjected to in his cell. He couldn't change the station and he couldn't even control the volume. Much of the programming from ten PM and seven AM were infomercials. Sid knew all Ron Poppeil's spiels by heart. On Sundays, it was all Church all the time as the fundamentalist preachers in the area used that station for a pulpit. The rest of the programming was syndicated reruns shown over and over. Most of them produced and directed by Aaron Spelling. Sid was mind blown by the choices available from the TV in his room in the hospital. The orderlies bought him the premium package. The amazing array of choices paralyzed him.

He turned it on, but couldn't get beyond the menu. When the urologist returned, Sid was still scrolling through the menu.

"Are you ready for your capacity test, Sid? "

"I guess so."

"This will be fairly easy. I am going to take this bag of sterile saline and hang it on your IV pole. I am going to hook the hose to the end of your catheter. I want you to tell me when you feel that your bladder is full. In the meantime, I am going to measure how much saline it takes to make you feel full. I have never used more than half a liter. Then I am going to measure the amount that comes out when I hang the bag on the bed frame. It should be the same, or slightly more. Are you ready?"

The fluid ran down the tube into the catheter. The urologist went out into the hallway and brought in an ultrasound machine. He greased a spot above the bladder and turned on the machine. At first, he couldn't find the bladder. It had been so long since it had been full, that it had shrunk and flattened. As it filled, it became easier to see. He watched it expand on the screen of the ultrasound machine.

"O K stop! It's full"

"I see you can feel it."

"It's been a long time, but yes."

"Does it hurt at all?"

"No, it just feels like I have to pee."

"O k, that was three hundred ccs."

"Now, I am going to take the bag off and drain your bladder into this graduated flask. Tell me if you can feel the fluid going out."

"I can feel my bladder shrinking."

"Now, try to squeeze down."

"I can't."

"Not at all?"

"Nope!"

"Ok, that answers my questions on several things."

"I don't think I want to know what those questions are."

"I'm just glad I didn't make any promises about normal urination."

"Oh."

"It's not that bad though. You have almost

normal bladder capacity and you can tell if it's full. That means that you won't have to have a second bag for urine unless you end up in a wheelchair. I'll be back tomorrow morning to see you. I have to think about some things."

He wrote on the chart and left the room. Shortly afterwards, a nurse came in and gave him a sponge bath. The attention felt good. She applied salve to the rash and changed the bags on the IV stand. About the time she finished, an orderly came in with a bowl of beef broth and some Jell-O. It was ten o'clock. Sid returned to his TV choices. He never realized that there was so much available. With the addition of cable TV, time melted. It was time for the procedure. The staples were pulled out. The tuck in the skin on his thigh held fast. The plastic surgeon declared him ready. The urologist declared him ready. The Foley catheter was removed and replaced with a simple catheter instead. The GI surgeon declared him ready. The lower GI revealed a healthy clean colon. He was prepped and sedated. He was woozy under the sedative, and still excited at the prospects. He was wheeled into the operating room where a group of sixteen individuals would be performing something that they had declared impossible three years before. The surgeons went through the identity and pre-operation protocol with Sid. He assented as well as he could. The team checked the paperwork one more time and set to work. When they started separating the mucous membrane from the skin around the orifice, the plastic surgeon said, "That work looks familiar, I have seen that stitching line a thousand times in my patients. I know the lady that did that. She used to do my closures and all my lip stitching. Look how the juncture seems natural. The scar at the division is almost microscopic. Not a day goes by that I wish she was back in my OR. Her little hands were magical. Her stitches were small, tight, and even. The edges never buckled and there was rarely any scarring. The hospital laid her off against my arguments. She was Asian. The hospital didn't have a racial quota for them so they laid her off for a black and a Mexican new hire to balance some politically correct quota. I wonder what happened to drive her to this."

"It must have been pretty bad. That is a very angry tattoo on his forehead. It hasn't faded at all. This isn't the kind of thing I would imagine her doing. She's the little Vietnamese girl that could predict what you needed and have it ready before you asked for it. She worked in my OR too, occasionally. She was a really nice girl. Best OR nurse a surgeon could ask for. I can't imagine her, getting that angry."

"Look at this stoma!"

"It's perfect!"

"It looks natural"!

Yeah, no danger of back flow at all. The protrusion is perfect. So is the angle."

After they dissected the urethra from the rectal wall, they cut off a slice of the rectum to use for other purposes. They used the piece with the stoma for a peritoneal wall after first removing the mucosa from it. A strip was cut off the edge of the remaining piece and handed to the urologist. He folded it in half and stitched up the edge. He then turned the mucosa inward by turning the piece inside out. It ended up as a tube with a three-centimeter diameter. In the meantime, the GI surgeon was performing a colostomy with the end of the rectum. After he finished, the urologist sewed the tube onto the stump of the urethra.

"Hey guys, she left us the valve. It was farther upstream than usual."

"It would be nice if it worked after all this. The nerve is missing from it. It's relaxed. Here's the nerve bundle. It doesn't look good. Here's the attachment point for it. It looks like she nicked it removing the prostate. It's a common mistake in prostate surgery. It always leads to incontinence. Let's stitch it together and hope for the best."

"Yeah, it shows that without magnification, she did an amazing job."

"I would have needed magnification for that stoma."

"You're an old man! You need magnification for everything!"

The GI specialist stitched the strip of ex rectum to the side of the peritoneum in the incision. He cut a hole in the middle and pulled the new urethra through it and clamped it. He then went around the rest of the incision, making sure that there would be no wrinkles in the edges. As it got blood flow again, it pinked up.

"I'll bet that that's the first time outside of a MASH unit that that has been done."

"That's amazing. That's all capillaries."

"No it's not. I just found vessels and joined them where I could. There are a lot of them in both the peritoneum and the colon wall. It only took a little bit of stretching to line them up with each other. In the battlefield conditions, they did it without magnification with about a forty percent success rate, working through intestinal contents. Here we have ideal conditions."

The plastic surgeon took over. He cut off the tuck from Sid's thigh and flattened it out. He folded the skin side inward and stitched it to retain some crease when it flattened out. He lined it up with the urethra and cut a small hole in the crease. Using very fine suture and adhesive he made a tiny stoma in the bottom of the crease. He pulled the hemostat off the urethra and lined up the edges He centered the crease on the pubic arch and put two stitches in

to center it. He did the same with the coccyx area.
He stretched the flap to the thighs and put a couple
of stitches to center it. He then secured the piece of
skin into place. When he was finished, Sid had a
natural fold concealing the urethra. It would look
perfectly natural after some healing. After six and a
half hours, Sid was wheeled into recovery. After
about an hour, Sid started to waken. It seemed very
cold to him. He shivered and shook in his
grogginess. He was disoriented and shaky. A nurse
came and took his vital signs. He instinctively
reached down. His groping fingers found a
colostomy bag beside his navel. He reached down
farther, and found a bandage with a catheter
protruding through it. He felt a tightness in his
crotch. He was out of surgery and the orifice that
had plagued him for three years was gone. He had a
pelvic floor again. He felt sick to his stomach and
needed to vomit. Nothing came out. He gagged and
heaved. A nurse came and put something into his

Covenant Roman Catholic Church

IV. The retching stopped like magic. After a couple of hours, he was rolled back into his room. He found flowers, a balloon and a card. He had a visitor.

38 Heard it Through the Grapevine

Marjorie still had a love for the Vanderbilt plastic surgery unit. She still had ties with some of the people there. Some of it was third or fourth hand communication, but she still got news of anything that would interest her. She still missed the sometimes-cutting edge work they did there. Most of all, she missed the legitimacy that work in that unit brought her. She got involved early on in all the difficult and challenging cases. Her sewing skills were legendary there. Her small hands could do things that a male surgeon found impossible. Her sharp eyes could pick out details that better trained surgeons would routinely miss. No surgeon ever had a malpractice suit when she was in the OR as they would defer the really tough stitchery to her. She was a closing specialist. She had been involved in the controversial artificial cartilage project where ear cartilage would be formed out of plastic and encased in flesh. Most of the patients were burn victims. Ears tend to burn off in fires. The Vanderbilt unit was synthesizing ears on a pilot project. Relatives came out of the woodwork to complain. The early ears looked straight out of a comic book. It was Marjorie that made the breakthrough with the plastic armature to support the skin. It enabled the patients to wear glasses if they needed them and were a lot less trouble than the stick-on silicone variety, which would fall off at in-opportune moments, usually dropping the eyeglasses to the floor. The relatives claimed that they were unsightly, even though the earless profile of the pre-surgical patient was even more unsightly. They sued and Vanderbilt shut down the program before a single claim was litigated. Shortly afterward, Marjorie was laid off in a staff restructuring brought about by a civil rights lawsuit by an affirmative action group. She was let go, because there wasn't a big constituency for south East Asians, especially Vietnamese. Had she been

Chinese, she might have been able to stay. Because of the sudden shutdown of the controversial experimental program that she was involved in, no other hospital wanted to hire her, even with the skills she brought to the table. She answered a magazine ad and became the triage nurse at Sterling College. She had lots of friends and supporters at Vanderbilt, but Sterling Forks was eighty miles south and she didn't drive. Her grape vine was made up of friends and relatives of nurses and orderlies still active at Vanderbilt. If it was big news around the hospital, she heard it. Practicing as an underground surgeon kept her skills sharp. Her patients were people who for one reason or another wouldn't seek medical care from an accredited physician. Her specialty was gunshot wounds and other violence induced injuries. It was always done in a primitive environment for cash or trade goods. It paid well and she didn't have to punch a clock or deal with office politics. She once resectioned an intestine that was severed in three places by a machete. It was an all-nighter and she was lucky. The patient was a cocaine dealer and he paid her handsomely in cash after he Recovered. Nobody ever saw his girlfriend, who swung the machete, again. The grapevine was also her source of medical supplies for cash, no questions asked. Her anesthesia of choice was Novocain, administered spinally, in major cases or locally in minor stuff like bullet removal from extremities. In spite of the long odds and primitive conditions, she never lost a patient due to her work. Several of her patients were shot dead later, but nobody died because of her work.

When the news came down the grapevine about the experimental reconstruction of the pelvic floor of a convicted rapist, she had to get involved. It was her hospital, and she was responsible for the missing pelvic floor as well as its contents. She knew the surgical team and the patient. She had visited him in prison to seek his forgiveness and to forgive him for raping her, even though the rape had all but destroyed her, and the missing pelvic floor was her revenge for it. She needed to reassure him that there was hope after it was over and he wasn't going back into the loveless world that he was emerging from. She had seen the magazine articles. Her tattoo was still stark and sharp on his forehead. She threw up when she turned the page and saw the picture. Here was permanent evidence of her anger and hurt. She had gotten over it, but Sid was marked forever. She bought a round-trip bus ticket to Nashville. On her way from the bus station to Vanderbilt, she stopped at a florist and made an order. She knew from all the years of nursing, that there is nothing sadder than going from the OR to an undecorated room. She had them delivered and headed across town. She hadn't been in town for a while. A lot had changed. As she walked she reacquainted herself to a beloved place. She took a circuitous route past the St Thomas hospital. She had feelings for that place too. She walked through the Vanderbilt campus with the students loitering about. She walked into the lobby and she felt like she was home. She forgot how much she missed the place, even though her departure was not as nice as she would have liked. She was only in the room for a couple of minutes when the orderlies rolled Sid back into the room. The reunion was tearful as both people had a lot of emotion over their strange relationship.

"I heard about your surgery, and had to make sure you were Ok."

"I'm so happy you came to see me."

"I want to look at that tattoo. I have someone who may be able to help you in Lynchburg."

"Can you make this thing go away?"

"I think, most of it."

"Why?"

"I have a lot of regrets about what I did. I got sick when I saw your picture in Time."

"I don't see it; it doesn't bother me."

"I was angry. It was a final parting gesture. There is a whole bottle of black tattoo ink in that thing. I went over it and over it. It was bleeding when I finished it."

"It really doesn't bother me, honest!"

"It haunts me in my dreams."

"Look, it helps me in my work with the kids. It freaks them out. I lost the lower part today. I need it as a reminder of the things I did out of hurt and anger in my life. Just let it be."

"Are you sure?"

"I probably won't ever see the outside again. I shouldn't be there anyway. This mark on my forehead sets me apart. It marks me for the terrible things I have done to countless people. I was evil. I deserve it, not for what I did to you, but what I did to others who never got the chance for a day in court. I wear it proudly."

Covenant Roman Catholic Church

"You're fucked up, Sid! You are really fucked up. I guess I am too. If there's anything I can do for you, I want to do it."

"You already have, you showed up and cared about me. You turned my life around. In all my life, nobody else ever did."

39 Deidre and Corinne Bury the hatchet

Louie answered the door and greeted a strange young woman. She was obviously in a bad way. Her clothes were rumpled and she was barefooted. She had a pocket book and a gym bag. She looked tired and worn. She was also very thin, and under a sunburn, very pale.

"Is this still the Slackmeyer residence?' she asked.

"Yes, it is."

"Thank God, I thought someone else owned the place now."

"No, this is still the Slackmeyer residence, and you are?"

"Deidre. I grew up here."

"Oh, you're the other daughter. I have heard about you, but not very much. Come in!"

Deidre walked into the house. Not much had changed in her absence. It was still huge and full of echoes. She loved playing with the echoes as a child. The front hallway was special, as the echo was almost as loud as the original sound. Beyond that, there weren't very many happy memories. She was Miranda's whipping child. If anything happened Deidre would get punished. The memories still ached. The little man that greeted her seemed very nice so she relaxed a bit. As she walked from the front hallway into the living room, Charlene appeared at the top of the stairs in a white terry cloth robe, with a towel around her hair. When Deidre saw her, her face got even paler and she screamed. She dove under a table and curled up into a ball.

"No, Mama, No", she whimpered. "You're dead, I know you're dead!"

"What's the matter?" asked Louie.

"I thought she was dead. I know I missed her funeral, but everyone told me she was dead!"

"Who's dead?"

"She got hit by a train and shredded. They told me!"

Louie looked up and saw Charlene, who was totally mystified by the behavior of the strange woman in the living room. Then, Charlene remembered Ben's reaction to her when he met her.

"You must be Deidre. I know, I look like your mother. Everyone tells me that. Hey, look, I have red hair. I'm Charlene. I'm here to take care of your dad."

Charlene took the towel off her head and a cascade of wet red hair fell out of it. Deidre wept uncontrollably under the table. Her entire body was shaking. This woman sounded a little like Mama too. Then she realized that Mama would be a lot older. This woman was, maybe her own age, or close to it. She started to laugh. She crawled out from under the table.

"You scared me half to death!" You look just like my mother did at the time I left home."

Covenant Roman Catholic Church

"I get that a lot around here."

"Where's Dad?"

"He's asleep already."

"Yeah, it's late."

"You look like you walked through Hell,
Girl. How did you get here? I didn't hear a car."

Covenant Roman Catholic Church

"I walked from town."

"Barefooted?"

"Well, I did start out with shoes"

"What happened to them?"

"One of them came apart, about a mile from the bus station."

"Where are you staying?"

"I'm homeless."

"Homeless? What do you mean?"

"About four months ago, my husband died. He left me without any savings.' I lost our apartment. What little we owned is in storage in Memphis. There is a little money from royalties supporting the rent on it. I was strung out on coke. I went to Betty Ford and got dried out. It took the last money I had. The bus trip back finished me. I came here, because I had no place else to go."

"You're home now. You won't ever be homeless again. Your dad will be so glad to see you. So will your sister."

"She's here?"

"She walked in here much like you did, but with two kids."

"I can't stay here."

"Why not?"

"Because she's here."

"What do you mean?"

"Mom always liked her best. We haven't gotten along since I was in seventh grade. We fought over everything.""What do you mean?"

"She didn't want me around. She wanted to be the only daughter. She did things to me."

"What did she do?"

"I don't want to talk about them. I have a warrant out on me because of her."

"What do you mean, a warrant?"

"If I get caught around here by the cops, I'm subject to arrest."

"You were a teenager when you left here, how could you have done something to cause them to have a warrant on you?"

Covenant Roman Catholic Church

"All I am going to say is there was this boy
that Corinne was dating. We got in trouble together.
We were into drugs, Corinne too, and the money
had to come from somewhere."

"You did criminal stuff for money for drugs,
when your parents had all this?

"Mom never gave us any money. We
weren't allowed to shop by ourselves. We wore
what she told us to, or there would be hell to pay."

'Why didn't I ever hear about this? Your dad
never said anything. He said that he came home one
day to find Corinne gone, and then a couple of years
later, you. He could never understand why."

"The cops came looking for us. Mama told
them that her perfect daughters, actually she didn't
use that word, but she implied it, would never do
such a thing. After dealing with Mama, they went
away."

"But why are you holding a grudge against
each other?"

Covenant Roman Catholic Church

"She threw me under the bus to the cops when they came to school to question her."

"Why is she holding a grudge against you?

"I told Mama."

"What happened then?"

"Mama put her head through the wall and then cut off all her hair."

"Now I understand your reaction when you saw me coming down the stairs."

"I was terrified. It was extremely hard to come here. I was in ninth grade when I left here. I lied about my age, and ran off with a saxophone player from Memphis. I had been sneaking off to the college at night. That's where I was getting my drugs."

"I understand. I'll bet you're hungry."

"I had a hamburger in Omaha, yesterday."

"Is that all?"

"I didn't have any more money. I had to panhandle to get that. It was a degrading and humiliating experience. I just couldn't bring myself to do it again."

"Let's find you some food."

They retired to the kitchen. Charlene and Louie prepared a grilled cheese sandwich and a bowl of soup. Deidre ate only half of the sandwich and a third of the soup.

"I can't eat any more. It's good, but I haven't been eating much. They were worried about me at Betty Ford, because I only weighed eighty-eight pounds. I wasn't eating much before, then my husband died. I kept forgetting to eat. I don't think that the cocaine helped either. We had just scored an ounce the day before he passed. When he passed, I don't remember eating until I got light headed while I was scattering his ashes along Beale St. At Betty Ford, they were always forcing me to eat."

"Don't you get hungry?"

"Not really."

"You really need to eat."

"I know, I just kept forgetting until I stopped feeling hunger. I wait until I get lightheaded, then I eat a little. It's been that way for a couple of years."

"Did your husband know about it?"

"I don't think he really cared. His loves were music and cocaine. I really never fit into the equation. I was just another piece of clothing. It got worse when our daughter died."

"You had a daughter?"

"Yeah, she was beautiful. She had a *cafe au lait* complexion and big expressive brown eyes. She had black wavy hair and a dancer's figure. I have pictures in Memphis. I really miss her. I wish I had died instead of her."

"How old was she?"

"Twelve."

"Omigod, she was just a child. I'm so sorry!"

"She lingered in a coma for a while. We had so much hope, but she never woke up."

"Did you tell your dad?"

"It would have killed him. He never knew we had a child. I was selfish. I wanted no contact with home."

"Was it that bad here?"

"Has Corinne said anything?"

"She never talks about the past."

"How is she with the kids?"

"They laugh a lot and run through the house. I love the sound of it and so does your dad."

"I'm glad that they have a healthy relationship. I had one like that with Sonia. That was the name of my girl. I allowed her to be a child, to be whatever she wanted to be. I raised her with the idea that we are all works in progress and it's ok to make mistakes. I wish you could have heard her sing.

Deidre started to cry.

"I thought I was done crying, dammit!"

"It doesn't work that way. Besides, you haven't yet started mourning your husband."

"That didn't hurt as much. After Sonia died, he lost the will to live. I could hear it in his music. He was a broken man. He had a child with a white woman. His daughter had a chance to be somebody like he never felt capable of being."

"He really must have loved her."

"She meant the world to him."

"How did you end up like this?"

"Cocaine. It's what brought us together and what destroyed us. We were casual users, a line here and there around the clubs. He said it opened his soul so the music could flow out. After Sonia died, we both self-medicated our grief with it. We used more and more. When he passed, we had just started a fresh ounce. After he died, I finished the ounce. When it got toward the end, I realized that there would be no more ounces… ever. There was no more money and no more income. I don't think he really loved me. I was basically an arm decoration to trot around the clubs like a show horse. I really don't think he was capable of love toward a woman. He loved his daughter though. After she died, life in the apartment was as bad as it was here, but I was too proud to come home. I couldn't deal with the shame. Besides I was hooked on coke. After he died, I knew in order to face Dad, I had to be clean and sober. I didn't want to be like Mama."

"What do you mean?"

"The only times she was sober was when Dad was due in. She had trouble doing even that. She was a mean drunk, mean and demanding. She beat us. We were terrified of her."

"Is that why you freaked out in the living room?

"Yes. I thought she came back from the dead to punish me for losing a husband and a daughter, and for marrying a black man. There were some good times with him. His family accepted me. They were very nice people."

Covenant Roman Catholic Church

"Is that why Corinne changes the subject when I mention her mother?"

"I'm sure of it."

"I'm seeing a picture here. Does your dad   - know any of the mess here at home?"

"I don't think so. We were sworn by forfeiture of our lives to secrecy."

"Does your brother know?"

"He swore the same oath. We took the brunt of it though. He assured us that he would be O K after we left. He was six feet tall and two hundred and fifty pounds in seventh grade. We took him to his word."

"Didn't he play football for Vanderbilt?"

"Full Scholarship, free ride. He hated playing pro. He quit after a season with Philadelphia. Too many concussions."

"You have to stay here tonight. Your dad will want to see you!"

Covenant Roman Catholic Church

"I really have no choice, unless you want to drive me to the homeless shelter in Lynchburg."

"That's not an option. Your old room is just how you left it, except I have been dusting, so it is probably cleaner and the bed is made up."

"Thank you. I'll go up to bed now. I'm spent!"

When Deidre woke the next morning, it was as if she had traveled in time. It was like the past years never happened. Her school books were on her desk, open to where she left them. The same poster was on the wall. She jumped from the feeling. When she opened her eyes. It was bright daylight outside. She got out of bed and went into the bathroom. As she sat on the toilet, she looked around. Her makeup was still on the vanity. When she eloped, she hadn't returned home from the campus. She simply climbed into his car and rode to Memphis. She went to her closet and selected some clothing. It was loose on her. She weighed less than she did as a high school freshman.

Covenant Roman Catholic Church

"I have got to start eating regularly", she muttered to herself, as she looked at herself in the mirror. The image in the mirror belied the appearance of her surroundings. The high school freshman had become a middle-aged junkie. She emptied the makeup out of her pocket book onto the vanity and tried to fix it. She didn't want her dad to see her like that. Her cheeks were hollow. She had bags under her eyes. Her hair was thin and wispy. The skin on her neck sagged. As she worked on the foundation, she tried to erase the sorrow lines around her mouth. After about half an hour, she felt presentable enough to venture downstairs. There were certainly limits to what could be done with makeup. The sallowness of her complexion was eased somewhat. The wrinkles were eased a little, but she still looked older and sicker than she wanted to. She had definitely outgrown the style of clothing she was wearing. It was too young for a woman of her age, and of the wrong era. She had no choice, because the clothing in the gym bag was in need of washing and she had lived in busses and slept in what she had arrived in for four days. With great trepidation, she descended the stairs and headed for the kitchen. The youngish man and an older woman were discussing the merits of a merger on the financial page of the newspaper. The voice of the older woman sounded familiar.

"Dad?"

"Deidre! You've come home!"

Both of them started crying. Neither one could talk. So much had happened since they last saw each other. Both of them said at the same time, "What happened to you?"

"Dad, you are a woman!"

"Yeah, cancer does that sometimes."

"I have so much I need to tell you. I'm sorry I never communicated. After a couple of years, I was so ashamed of myself for disappearing, I couldn't face you. Please forgive me!"

"I have always loved you and hoped and prayed for your return. You've come back to me. That's all that matters. Forgive me for being an absentee parent. I know now from talking to your sister, that things weren't easy for you during my absences. I'm so sorry. Please forgive me!"

Both of them laughed as they hugged each other tears flowed. Makeup ran. Louie sliced a bagel and put it into the toaster.

"Do you want butter or cream cheese? "

"I'll take butter."

Deidre poured herself a cup of coffee, put an ice cube into it and sat down at the table.

"Black?"

"Yeah, we ran out of milk one day, and I discovered that I like it better as just coffee."

"It's funny, your mother tried for years to make me put milk and sugar into mine. On the road, I always drank it black. Louie still ruins his."

All three of them laughed.

"I think you need to go visit Iggy."

"Yeah, nothing here fits me."

"Usually, when a woman tries to put on clothing that she wore in school, it's too small. I've never seen it the other way."

"Yeah, it was a wakeup call for me too. I have to remember to eat."

Tim came into the kitchen to get something out of the refrigerator.

"Hey Gramp, who is the lady?"

"This is your Aunt Deidre."

"I have an aunt? I have an aunt!"

"She's going to be staying here."

"Cool! I'll go tell Ma."

He ran out of the kitchen and upstairs.

"Hey Ma, Aunt Deidre's here!"

There was the sound of a ceramic object breaking on the floor followed by the sound of six running feet. Corinne and her children came into the kitchen.

Covenant Roman Catholic Church

"You're here", said Corinne icily.

'Yeah, I'm here."

"You said you'd never come back after Mama
died."

"I'm sorry I disappointed you, but I had to, I
ran out of options."

"What happened? Did the nigger kick you out
because you got old and skinny?

"No, He died!"

There was a long stunned silence. Deidre
started to cry again.

"What happened? Did that worthless idiot biker
kick you out because you got fat?"

There was another thick silence. Corinne
started to cry too. They fell into each other's arms and
embraced as sisters, both of them wept bitterly.
Corinne's children watched in puzzled silence.

Covenant Roman Catholic Church

40 The Jesuit Convocation

With great reluctance, Fred decided to say yes to
Father Bob's invitation to the convention of the
American Jesuit Congress, which was being held this
year in Birmingham. He was to be a guest speaker. He
wasn't terribly sure, as he was in his soul, still on the
Orthodox side of conservative. Christianity was still
foreign and Catholicism was still somewhat suspect
because of history. He liked Father Bob and his
message. He knew that Christianity was simply
distilled and applied Judaism. He was suspicious of the
hierarchical nature of the Church. Judaism has no real
hierarchy. It is centered on the local shul. The local
Rabbi was the authority. Beyond that was a huge
volume of decisions from individual rabbis and holy
men going back five thousand years. It was all written
down in a huge volume of work called the Talmud. An
observant Jew spends a lifetime studying it along with
the Torah, which stayed in its original language so that
translation into other languages wouldn't alter it by the

nuances of the different languages. The spiritual nature was secondary. He liked the spiritual nature of Christianity. It was the missing link in his faith. He knew many Jews that didn't reflect on spirit at all. They just studied and obeyed the many laws without ever reflecting on the spiritual aspect of Judaism as well as other religions. The Rabbi that taught him as a child was one of them. Yet here he was, speaking to a large group of priests and archbishops about the basic faith of Jesus Christ and the original language in the Eucharist, and how when he heard it celebrated the first time, found the incredible power of the Holy Spirit, as it washed through him during the Invocation. It was the thing that was missing in his faith. Here was incredible power. It called to his very soul. This was the thing that Father Bob wanted him to express to the group. Only a Jew could bring forth this interpretation. Two small groups of words in Hebrew, blessing the bread and wine, just as Jesus spoke them at the first Eucharist brought it all home. Simple sentences spoken at every mealtime by every Jew on the planet. Jesus was a Jew, just like him. His offense was rejecting the hierarchy that grew around the Temple in Jerusalem. He rejected that, and the slavish micro observance of the hundreds of sometimes conflicting laws governing every aspect of life. They were impossible to totally observe because of their very number. The discipline involved was the backbone of an ancient and beautiful tradition. In the truly observant, there was an underlying joy in the mitzvah of being observant. In the back of his mind, he both envied and resented the ultra-orthodox sects. Charlene drove. Charlene and Marjorie were invited along because they had introduced Fred to Father Bob, and Charlene had access to a car.

Charlene had her own trepidations. It was the first trip out of town since her departure from the college faculty. Except for a couple of small errands into town, it was the first time she had been away from the house since she moved in. She would be among a

389

large group of people, mostly men for an extended period of time. It was all she could do to maintain her composure in the car enough to drive. How would she handle a convention? Her heart raced. Her palms were sweaty. Her arm pits dripped perspiration that ran down her sides. It was hard to concentrate on the road to Birmingham. The car she was driving belonged to a dead woman who still inhabited her every waking minute. The man who survived her was now a woman. The only man she had ever really connected with was in the process of becoming one, because he was born a woman. They had so much in common. They both went to Quinnipiac. They were both raised in Connecticut. They liked the same literature, and were both contemplative loners. She had a biological urge to settle down and raise a family. She wasn't sure what Louie wanted as she lacked the courage to ask him. Louie still needed to find a surgeon capable to modify his body into manhood. Straight answers were scarce as that facet of plastic surgery was new and unpublicized. It was all so confusing. It was territory she had never thought to explore. Nothing she had read in her vast explorations of literature prepared her for this conundrum. She still hated and feared men, yet she wanted one in the worst way. Why was the one she found originally a woman? How does the biblical prohibition against homosexuality apply here? In the meantime, she was going to a Catholic convention where such things aren't even imagined, with a charismatic priest, a has been bestselling author, and his girlfriend. Oldies played softly on the radio. A single tear ran down Charlene's cheek. How could her orderly over managed and planned life go so far off the track?

Marjorie was asleep. Her head rested against the door of the car. She had been up all night repairing the damage from a botched castration at the tattoo parlor in Lynchburg. The castration was successful, but the collateral damage required her surgical skills and her discretion. It had paid well, but she almost lost the patient from loss of blood. It gnawed at her. Someday she would run out of luck and be prosecuted for practicing medicine without a license. She had repaired knife wounds, impalements, and gunshot wounds in primitive environments. Every one of them was done in an environment of secrecy. It was telling on her. She was good at it. So far, nobody had died. A car would pick her up at all hours and take her to the patient. She would make the needed intervention, and ride back to Fred's place. Fred knew better than to ask where she had gone, because Marjorie was supporting him with the money earned from this highly illegal impromptu medicine. As she slept, she dreamed of being a little girl playing with paper dolls in an anonymous hotel lobby and watching the stream of guests flow through. There were people of all shapes sizes and colors flowing anonymously through her life. Most of them seemed friendly. She wasn't allowed to make contact, so she played quietly with her paper doll book and her scissors, and observed the flow of humanity. She was an only child and there were no playmates in the stream flowing before her. She was lonely. The paper dolls were an imaginary family that she made up stories about. They were her family. She dressed them up for all manner of occasions. She still after many years dreamed about the time among the paper dolls. Sometimes in her dreams the dolls came to life and talked to her. She cherished these dreams. It never bothered her that the dolls didn't look like her. They were their own family that shared their lives with her. They didn't have to look like her. They lived in nice homes, not in a hotel room that changed from week to week. Her favorite paper doll book had the nice home in it. She would open it up and move the dolls around in the nice home. She watched the tourists too. The scene morphed into the plastic surgery O R at Vanderbilt. She helped surgeons change people's lives by fixing things. Her paper doll people would have wounds repaired on their faces, have missing breasts replaced, or have the indignities of aging reversed.

They would be happy paper doll people. Or happy hotel tourists. The scene would shift to the back room of a tattoo parlor, where an attempt at a body modification would go terribly awry and she would fight to slow the disfigurement or stem the bleeding. She moaned in her sleep. She was sick of repairing people's sons and daughters who on a lark decided that some body parts were expendable, and chickened out halfway through the procedure. It showed in her dreams. The body parts kept getting bigger until she was dealing with arms and legs. She screamed. It came out as a yip as she jerked awake.

"Good morning sunshine."

"I gotta find another line of work."

"That bad?"

"Yeah."

"We're almost there."

"I'm sorry I crashed on you."

"That's OK, The scenery's nice."

"I'm sorry that I've been such a stranger lately."

"Hey, that's OK, I've been too busy to notice."

"How's our patient?"

"Except for becoming a woman…OK. It's been a year and a half, and no sign of the cancer."

"I mean mentally. Last time I saw him he was a mess."

"His daughters moved in with us."

"How's that going?"

"It's nice having people in the house."

"Oh?"

"Yeah, one of them brought her kids. It's nice."

"Nice?"

"Yeah, with just the two of us, it was lonely. We didn't see each other for days at a time."

"I can see that."

"Now there's seven of us."

"Seven?"

"Yeah. Me, Ben, Corinne, Deidre, Tim, Hope, and Louie."

"Who's Louie?"

"Ben brought him home from the stockholders meeting. He's teaching Ben how to properly present himself as a woman."

"How can a man teach another man to present himself as a woman?"

"Easy, he used to be one."

"OK…"

"He's really nice. We spend a lot of time together. He's from Greenwich."

"So. You got a boyfriend, now."

"Well…"

"Yeah, you're sweet on him, aren't you, I can tell."

"Let's say that I'm conflicted. He used to be a woman. I'm sorta having problems with that. I thought a romantic relationship would lead to children."

"You're more than friends?"

"Yeah, we've fooled around a bit."

"You? Getting frisky… with a man?"

Charlene giggled and blushed.

Covenant Roman Catholic Church

"Not in front of a priest."

"OK."

Father Bob and Fred Laughed. They got off the highway and drove through the streets of Birmingham. Charlene hadn't driven in a city since she moved south. It took every bit of her concentration to avoid disaster. It was better than New Haven or Bridgeport, but not much. The traffic was erratic and frustrating. She was relieved when she pulled up in front of the hotel. Marjorie went in and secured two rooms. A bellman helped with the luggage. Soon they were unlocking rooms. The men took one and the ladies took the other. Charlene showered and put on fresh clothing. She put on her makeup and got ready to interact on a formal basis. She hadn't worn a dress except cotton sundresses since the rape in the park. She had chosen an n A line print with a mid-calf skirt from Miranda's collection for the trip. She admired herself in the mirror as she did her hair. It took a while because it hadn't been cut or styled for a couple of years. Marjorie wore her usual white blouse and black slacks.

"You say you have been more than friends with Louie."

"Let's just say that Ben's prosthesis works as advertised."

"Oh?"

"Louie wears it all the time. He says it's the one thing he was missing."

Marjorie laughed.

"I can imagine. It is seductive."

They both laughed

"I lost my fear of sex."

"Wow, I 'm so happy for you!"

"I didn't realize how wonderful it is. I think I'm in love!"

"Oh?"

"I haven't been gone for a day, and I miss him."

"Yeah, I guess you are. Let's go find the guys and see if we can be on time for the luncheon."

"OK. How do I look?"

"Better than I've ever seen you. Love must agree with you."

Charlene blushed and laughed.

"Let's go. The guys probably think we died in here."

They both laughed as they went out and shut the door. They found the men in the lobby. Fred and Father Bob were carrying on an animated discussion of the kosher dietary laws and the spirit behind them. Father Bob was fascinated. He had read the passages in Leviticus but Fred's description of the observance and the Yiddish description of actual mealtimes and kitchens fleshed out his understanding of something that had been glossed over in Seminary and his own study of Scripture. Father Bob studied Hebrew in seminary as an elective, but really didn't see the music in it until he met Fred. Fred was fluent. It was a native language to him. Father Bob understood the foundation of his faith. He knew his idea had merit.

Fred would ignite a whole new chapter in Catholicism. The Church was hurting. She was hemorrhaging membership. She was riddled with scandal and nepotism. She was timeworn. She was like the Temple when Jesus expelled the moneychangers. She was paralyzed by the hierarchy and hidebound old unimaginative leadership. The true Holy Spirit was lost in the shuffle, except in small out of the way congregations with charismatic priests that understood the Mandate. Father Bob was a Jesuit priest. He was proud of it. He was proud of the stubborn resistance to Papal authority over centuries, and the purity of the doctrine. At this conclave, there was a large group of Jesuits. History had marginalized the movement to the missions and to the poorest inner cities where the need was greatest. This marginalization had strengthened both the faith and resolve of the movement. As he listened to Fred's words the meaning of the movement hit home. The old ways had to go. There had to be a renewal, or the Church would implode from its own dead weight. It would be just like Jerusalem with the destruction of the second Temple and the following diaspora. The idea terrified him.

As he contemplated the chaos in his soul, he noticed the two women approaching. He was genuinely glad to see them. They provided some semblance of normalcy. In the testosterone fueled organization, he saw women as a balance wheel in a clock. They provided a link with reality and a spiritual foundation he was only just beginning to see. He greeted them both with hugs. He needed them near him more than he realized.

"Come on, Padre, it's lunch time!"

"I know. You ladies look great!"

"We need to look our best! We want to make a good impression, so our message gets heard."

"Yeah, it's still going to be hard to get their attention. They are too hung up on ritual and ceremony."

"Do you think that they will understand the Hebrew part of the message?"

"I don't know. Hebrew is an elective course in seminary."

They got in the car and drove to the Cathedral. There was a huge buffet set up in the basement. The room was full of people. There were a few lay people in the mix, but it was mostly priests with a few arch bishops thrown in. The Conclave drew from a region starting in Washington DC and reaching south to Florida and West to the Mississippi River. There were only about thirty women. Half of them were nuns. Only a few of them were wearing street clothes. This made Charlene really visible in her print dress. The bright colors glowed in the sea of black and white. That made her extremely nervous. She stuck close to Marjorie. They served themselves and sat down. They were late so they missed the blessing of the food. At the head table sat the

Cardinal and the Archbishops. The four from Sterling Forks found a table with four adjoining empty chairs and sat down. The room was loud with conversation, none of it about Church things. Only two people in the room were wearing yarmulkes. Fred had his black one, and the Cardinal wore a red one. Fred had trouble finding a suitable meal in the buffet. He ended up with a big salad and some fried chicken. Nothing else even came close to kosher. Charlene took a bowl of salad and a couple slices of bread. She was too nervous to think about food. Marjorie and Father Bob loaded their plates and ate lustily. Father Bob was in his element, and Marjorie enjoyed crowds.

The Archbishop from the Cathedral got up and called for attention. He introduced the Cardinal. The Cardinal got up and walked to the lectern. He leaned heavily on it. Marjorie didn't like the way he moved. She also didn't like his coloring. Because of his high position in the Church Hierarchy, the

Covenant Roman Catholic Church

Cardinal wore more clothing than the other clerics in the room. He was old. He had been in the priesthood for over forty years and moved up in the organization slowly. The Pope had chosen him for his political acumen and his ability to see both sides of an argument. Before he was called to the Priesthood, he had been studying law. He was a more than capable administrator and a fairly good public speaker. He swayed as he started to speak.

"Friends, fellow priests and bishops, and guests, we are here to talk about our mission and our relationship with each other and Jesus Christ. It's all intertwined. We need to interact with each other as we would interact with Jesus, because that is what he told us to do. That is our mandate as Catholics. To do less would be a disservice to both our fellow humans and Jesus."

He swayed on the lectern. His face grew more pale as he took a breath for more of his speech. Marjorie got up from her place at the table

404

and walked to the side of the room, heading for the head table. Fred and Charlene got up and followed. Father Bob reached into his jacket pocket for his tin of Chrism and followed. Everyone else in the room sat and patiently waited for the next sentence. The Cardinal wiped sweat from his forehead with a handkerchief and straightened himself.

"We make up only ten percent of the Catholic Church in America. We occupy almost a quarter of the landmass of the continent. We are competing with many other Christian churches as well as a plethora of other religions, all of them fiercely defended as the only true way by their practitioners. Our Mandate goes back to the upper room in Jerusalem, where Jesus Himself taught us how to find Him in the Eucharist. It is a hostile environment at best because we are also competing with the secular world of radio, TV, literature, and movies. We have to rise above that noise to get our message across."

He coughed and sagged against the lectern. His complexion was almost gray. He swayed more. He mumbled a prayer, and tried to take a deep breath. He struggled with it. He took a step sideways and fell face first to the floor. Marjorie was right there as soon as he hit the floor, Marjorie and Fred were rolling him over onto his back. Charlene ran into the kitchen and found a telephone. She dialed 911.

"Birminham diaspayach, what's y'all's emergency."

"We have a possible heart attack at the Cathedral. We need an ambulance and a paramedic."

"What's the address?"

"The Cathedral, you know, the big brownstone Catholic Church in the center of town."

"I need a street address Ma'am."

"I don't know it. It's the big brownstone church with all the statues out front and all the steps to the front door. Hurry!"

"Ma'am there are four cathedrals in the city of Birmingham, I need a street address."

"Please lady, I'm from Hamden Connecticut. I've never been to Birmingham in my life. It's the Catholic Cathedral and we have a man dying here. I am sure that someone in the building knows where we are by my description. Leave the space on the paperwork blank and send someone, please!"

"Yes Ma'am I'll send someone. Stay on the phone."

Marjorie cleared the airway. And started chest compression. Fred started mouth to mouth respiration. Father Bob started Last Rites. A policeman appeared. Another one appeared. Then a paramedic with a bag. He pulled out a stethoscope, and listened for a heartbeat. Fred continued the compressions. The paramedic pulled out a syringe and filled it and stuck it into the Cardinal's chest. Nothing happened. The paramedic had Fred stop the compressions while he took off the Cardinals robe, jacket and shirt. He let

Fred start again as he turned on the defibrillator. He rubbed the paddles together and read the meter. He stuck the paddles on the Cardinal's chest and yelled clear. Everyone jumped back. He sent the charge through the Cardinal's chest. The Cardinal jumped involuntarily as the huge charge went through his body. The paramedic checked for heart beat with his stethoscope. He told Fred to resume the compressions while he reset and recharged the defibrillator. Fred was getting tired and sore. Fifteen minutes had elapsed since the Cardinal fell over. An Oxygen bottle appeared Marjorie grabbed it and turned on the valve and used it instead of the mouth to mouth she was doing. She worked the bag and prayed quietly. Father Bob anointed the Cardinal, delivering the Extreme Unction in Latin. It felt better to him and he could feel the spirit move within him when he did it. The defibrillator made a hissing noise and smoke came out of it. The paramedic kicked it away in disgust and went out to get the spare from the ambulance. Fred kept doggedly pumping the Cardinal's chest. Finally, the atropine that the paramedic injected into the Cardinal's heart took effect. The Cardinal moaned and moved his legs. He coughed. Marjorie took the stethoscope and checked his heart. It was beating. It was ragged and irregular, but it was beating. Fred fell over backwards, drenched in sweat. He was exhausted. Marjorie fell across the cardinal and started to cry. Father Bob said a prayer of thanksgiving. Charlene hung up the phone. The paramedics took the Cardinal away on the stretcher. He was semiconscious, but alive. Fred picked up the red yarmulke from the floor and put it in his pocket.

Covenant Roman Catholic Church

Watch for Uprising

Covenant Roman Catholic Church

Does anyone actually know who they are?

Covenant Roman Catholic Church

About the Author

Jon Hykes was born in Pittsburgh, Pa was raised in
Murrysville Pa, spent time in the army after being
drafted. He traveled extensively as a musician and a
mechanic. He lived in Tennessee for a period of time
and spent time around Vanderbilt Hospital. Over the
years, he has been a tireless advocate on transgender
issues. He now lives in Connecticut.

Other works: *Who's Going to Say Kaddish for the
Chinaman's Dog, Poems from the Shop,* and
C:\COMPOST.

Covenant Roman Catholic Church

No extraterrestrials were harmed during the creation of this work.

Covenant Roman Catholic Church